Ceana

by TS Caladan

Pez Wars 3 - 1000 Years Later.

A New World has evolved from the ashes.

Edited by TS Caladan

Cover Art by TS Caladan

Published by TWB Press – www.twbpress.com

ISBN: 978-1-959768-18-0

Contents:

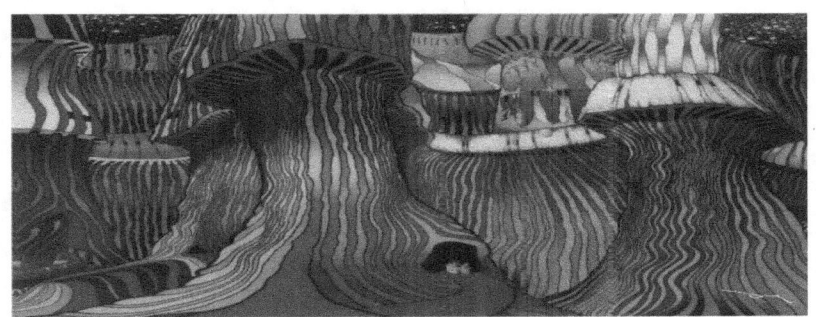

Dedicated

To

Fans

Of

Sci-fi,

Imagination

And

Truth...

and to my cat, Monkie.

TSC.

1 New World and Ceana

Ceana was a "proving-ground" over its millennial history, from pristine Paradise with only a few good people to a much larger population. The Gods watched the 'experiment' closely. Not the gods of the Milky Way. The highest of Authorities and almost all of the Archons were long gone. MONITORS, keen Observers, were from the highest realms of the Universe Above, the Next Level. "Upstairs." The real Giants.

Super Gods were no longer a matter of speculation and religious mysticism. They were factual and true. The most advanced creatures of the decimated galaxy understood to the smallest degree that they were watched like microbes in a glass dish. Some elites believed we were "in good hands" by caring/loving Parents. Then there were other great minds that thought *there could easily be another Galactic War, that just when Life has built itself back up into a huge anthill, there surely will be some force that will knock it back down again~*.

After the Great War, lifeforms in the galaxy flourished. Bits of Life expanded quickly. Aliens of all types procreated and produced various advances in technology. In the beginning and for the most part, the few were able to survive the Holocaust and survive well. Galactic masses were provided for by a number of "Care

Agencies" from worlds that still had abundance and lightspeed travel. 'Life found a way' and it grew and grew to staggering proportions a thousand years after the War.

In time, there was organization by responsible humans and aliens that were generally sick of war and the terrible devastation that went with it. They were constantly reminded, every single night, of what had happened a millennium ago. Imagine when you looked up into a clear night's sky and SAW ONLY A FEW STARS! The horrors in the aftermath of the ziggurats were always in plain view. You only had to look up to see a frightening new universe that surrounded everyone. No longer called the 'Milky Way,' the new galaxy was christened "Darkmoor" to those in many systems.

A major problem was there were not enough livable (M-class) planets and moons in a starfield that was so diminished. Darkmoor's growing overpopulation needed more and more fertile environments and such places were at a rare premium. There were once 100 billion stars in the Milky Way. Now, Darkmoor contains 3 billion suns. Of those 3 billion suns that remained, only 30 million systems supported human Life. Only 30 million in a space that once held 10 billion! Today, populated planets and moons were very crowded. Assistance and true answers were much needed as time marched on...

There was Hope. The Hope. She was the only female

Archon that survived the War. The only male Archon that still lived was Heart Center. Two. Only two Angels survived. They were the ones who took charge, organized, made changes and established a system of trade, commerce and relief to those in need. Archons piloted the ziggurats and also their counterparts, the Narchons. After the Great Explosions happened, only 3 ziggurats survived: The one driven by the Hope, the one driven by the Heart and one piloted by a Narchon. One demon-humanoid was still alive and it was their leader, the Dark Heart Center.

The galaxy healed and expanded and needed to expand more. Life needed livable environments and it certainly was possible for great minds of Darkmoor to manufacture planets, large moons and artificial satellites. BUT. Planet and satellite builders worked far too slow for what was required. It took more than 10-Earth years for a planet to "bake" or "cook" and become a habitat that harbored M-Class lifeforms. Populations BOOMED much faster than what was constructed. Soon, systems would reach a crisis point with dwindling food supplies and depleted energy sources.

*** *

Ceana was special, blessed and very much protected by gods and goddesses. Earth 2.0 was also *strange* because of Jefferson Douglas Blain's connection to it. He had been kept alive in a comatose state onboard what remained of the Rose Science Ship, which orbited the planet. The spacecraft, once the largest vessel in the galaxy, was whittled down to a diameter of 2000 miles and given an appearance identical to Earth's old Moon. Jeff's dream state formulated the matrix of Ceana, the people of Ceana as well as the nature of their society. A real, physical society of happy people. Jeff's subconscious memories, with the help of Max, produced a grand total of 20,000 original inhabitants of Ceana. Now there were millions. Millions of people that over generations had retained much of the original paradise. Overpopulation was not a problem on the New Earth.

A thousand years after the Great War, Ceana was spared much of the troubles and tribulations and horrors that other ET survivors experienced. Ceana was an actual utopia for hundreds of years. Today, not so much. Time, millions of people, and the exercise of FREEDOMS tarnished the utopia to a slight degree. Yet, after millennial celebrations were over, Ceana had little crime. Not only had there been no wars or conflicts where multiple deaths occurred...*there had not even been one murder!* The new planet had a history of Peace and this had been largely maintained over the centuries. Crime had been known to happen, rarely, but nothing too serious. There were magistrates that functioned as judges and settled local disputes that usually concerned marriages, divorces, property, petty thefts and other civil matters. 'The Eyes of the Above World' focused on the *experiment* of Ceana. So far, the 'glass dish' filled with *microbes* had been a raging success.

Anyone who lived on Ceana could go off-world by way of a space-transit system that appeared like huge PEZ dispensers. Most cities had these Launch Towers. Groups of space travelers, up to 100 passengers in a capsule, were propelled from the Towers, but not before a PEZ-head crown *slowly tilted back*. Towers spat capsules out of their top floor openings every 30 minutes. Passengers assembled inside the towers on different floors and lined up much as people would at amusement park roller coasters. Capsules mechanically moved up the towers as passengers waited for their car to be jettisoned out. A competent pilot commandeered each capsule like a bus driver. The rides into space were free. Everything was FREE on Ceana.

A number of destinations in space were possible, such as:

1) A large network of stations that orbited Ceana. These habitats were for higher education, recreation and entertainment.

2) Moon colonies. The core of the Rose Science Ship maintained an illusion that it was a satellite identical to Earth's Moon, only there were trees, plants, rivers, lakes, waterfalls and small oceans on its surface. The *mares* or

"seas" like Tranquility and Serenity were transformed into real seas. The air was artificial and natural and pure. There were seasons. Ice at the poles. The sky contained beautiful clouds. It rained in colors. There was different colored snow. Luna was referred to as the "Moon" and no citizen of Ceana understood its complex past history or what it actually was.

3) Mars colonies. Travelers to the red planet were usually interested in prehistoric ruins and visiting the world that brought forth the human race! The great archeological excavation of the "Face" and pyramids at Cydonia were prime locations for curious citizens.

4) People could visit the 4 Galilean moons of Jupiter. Not the surface of Io or Ganymede. Io was super volcanic and Ganymede was an unreal hologram [always was]. One could orbit Io from bases at safe distances. But the extremely popular moon of Jupiter was Callisto because of its subsurface ocean. Upon landing at port stations, a number of fantastic submersible vehicles were available for underwater exploration below the ice. Callisto contained undersea creatures beyond visitors'

wildest imaginations.

5) Saturn's Titan was an impressive metropolis and was a prime base to observe the incredible ringed-planet from various locations (other moons) and to venture to destinations beyond.

6) Pluto. [Earth's IAU declassified Pluto as "not a planet" or a "dwarf planet." This was because of the massive number of alien lifeforms that inhabited the planet and its complex satellite system hidden from the general public]. Visitors from Ceana and other worlds were highly welcomed by all the friendly and attractive aliens that were collectively known as Plutonians.

Small versions of the Launch Towers were located in cities and in each and every town on Ceana. Local transit systems shuttled many people or only a few people in comfortable capsules designed for air travel. The principle was the same: People gathered together and cued in line in buildings that resembled PEZ dispensers. In their capsules or cars, they rode up the buildings like elevators. The Head or whatever was on the building's roof moved back, then *the capsule was spat out,* one every five minutes. The rides were very safe and there was never a fatality.

Also, water travel was a similar situation. At various docks along rivers, lakes and oceans, there were cueing tunnels. Ceanans that desired to have an aqua-adventure, entered underground facilities at the docks. The finest restaurants were inside these public facilities and other (free) mall-type stores and services where nearly all your needs were met. After wonderful meals and shopping, people took leisurely boat rides. Or they had their choices of other sea vehicles that went very fast and underwater. Again, based on PEZ dispenser principles. The watercrafts lined up vertically and moved up until it was the capsule's turn to be expelled out from the top. Boats were gently pushed out to sea or were shot out like bullets from a gun. [No guns on Ceana].

Most everything major had a PEZ-twist to it because everything originated from the mind of PEZ-head, Jefferson Douglas Blain. Tall buildings in cities resembled giant stacks of PEZ candy in bubble packs.

The funny thing was: *PEZ candy, collecting dispensers and festivals that sold/traded the dispensers did not exist. They never existed on Ceana,* yet it seemed PEZ was everywhere and the planet itself had a sweet smell that affected everyone positively.

Food dispensers worked similarly. Food on this real planet was not like your normal foods on other real planets. You see, <u>SUGAR is a food that never spoils</u>. Truly. Sugar never spoils if it is kept dry. That [pez] principle was ingrained within every capsule of food. Yes, nourishment on Ceana consisted of colorful capsules or tablets of food from a few inches in length to more than one foot. The tablets or capsules were wrapped in clear cellophane that was not cellophane. (All plastic products were made from hemp, therefore biodegradable in time. Oceans contained no plastic or other pollutants). Various dispensers of different sizes were located in homes, in free service stores, in free restaurants or right on the street.

Food was extremely healthy and delicious because it came from a pure and natural source: *air and water.* There were no grocery stores, farms, gardens or the farming industry due to powerful "airators" and "waterators." Airators looked like radar dishes and were found on roofs of dome homes and large buildings. They *sucked in* huge amounts of air. Nutrients and what was known as *prana* were collected and condensed into food capsules in no time. All food on the planet were in this form of high-energy, "nourishment-bricks" that came in a wide assortment of colors and tastes.

Waterators operated the same way only they were placed at the end of long tubes that were submerged in rivers, lakes or oceans. Nutrients were pulled straight out of the water and were concentrated into delicious food pellets. There was too much food, yet obesity did not exist. Diseases, sickness, traditional hospitals and doctors did not exist. Everyone was intelligent and health-conscious and knew what to do because they were educated properly. Accidents and injuries were rare. If there was some tragic event, the usual robots were quickly dispatched and cleaned up the mess.

There was a robotic "Eye in the Sky" and similar systems in all cities and towns that *watched*. But this Artificial Intelligence Network CARED. It immediately predicted, saw and sent the proper response teams as if the system was an automatic 9-1-1. Artificial Intelligence Network or "Ain" was a good Big Brother.

Ceana's Sun was different than the Earth's Sun a thousand years ago. It was not blinding. The light was diffused, naturally, yet everything was brightly lit. Citizens could look directly at the Sun without any discomfort whatsoever. No glare. You didn't need to cover your eyes. Sunglasses were unnecessary and did not exist. [Glasses did not exist]. The effect was due to a *thick refraction element* in the atmosphere.

Technology controlled the weather. A lesser tilt of the planet's axis created seasons that only varied to a modest degree. The planet had no terribly cold, polar regions. The equator was comfortable because of the Sun's diffused light. [It was about the same conditions for all, citizens appeared to have the same skin color: a light tan]. The "Ain" system automatically produced different atmospheric conditions from day to day. Rain was produced precisely when and where rain was needed. There were no violent storms, lightning, hurricanes, tornadoes, twisters, high winds, tidal waves, volcanic eruptions or earthquakes! The Artificial Intelligence Network safely managed everything since the beginning. Mother Nature had not taken a single life on Ceana.

There were no cars, buses, planes, pollution or gas stations. There were only different sized sky-vehicles in the shape of (PEZ) capsules that transported people from Areas to Zones to Districts to Territories. Everyone, from the different Territories, considered themselves "Planetary Citizens," one race, one people. Together.

GAMES were very important to citizens. There were loads of cool games and things to do to occupy your days and nights. There was a reinvention of baseball called "Tri-Ball" that was anything but boring, designed for much higher scores. Baseball was exciting and played very quickly. Smaller field and only eight players on a team. More hits happened with only two infielders. A recessed infield favored hitters and not the pitcher. Sides changed after two outs. Four Strikes struck out a batter. Three Balls and batters took first base. Fouled off balls were Balls. So a pitcher only pitched a maximum of 6 pitches to any one batter. The new ballgame had no extra innings. If a game was tied, the best player from each team batted up in a tie-break situation.

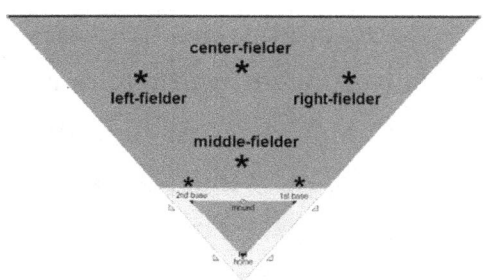

Big "stadias" surround many popular sports. Players and large numbers of fans parked their sky-vehicles in lots and attended the games with enthusiasm. Fights did not happen. It was good-natured sportsmanship. Everyone had a good time.

No one bet or drank alcohol at the Games. Yes, there was no desire for alcoholic beverages whatsoever on Ceana. People were naturally happy and did not need to be artificially-induced into happiness. Feelings were real.

Ceana

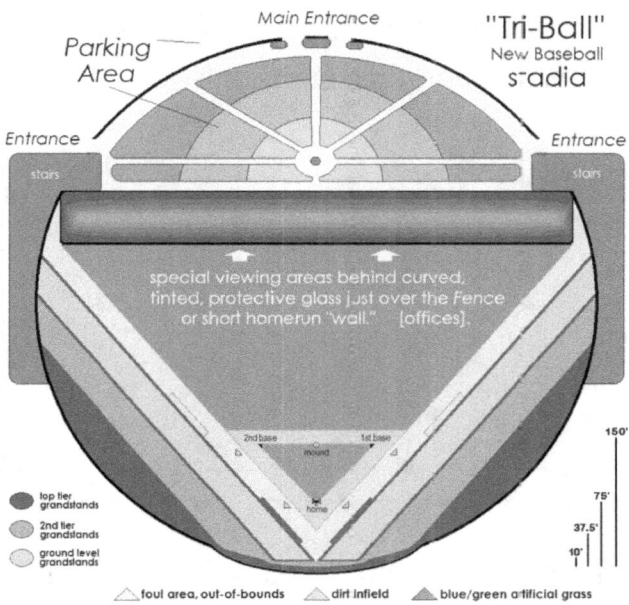

"Tri-Ball"
New Baseball
s-adia

Main Entrance

Parking Area

Entrance

Entrance

special viewing areas behind curved,
tinted, protective glass just over the Fence
or short homerun "wall." [offices].

Probably the most popular game on Ceana was Roval. Roval was a singles tennis court that had nothing straight. It contained No Lines! The Roval court could be described as a "stretched donut." It was longer than (Earth's) tennis courts by two feet. Servers were allowed to step into the court on serve. There were no foot-faults, lets or tie-breaks played. Ain system called the shots and it never made a mistake. Much of the (traditional) court was removed with no corners. The reason this elegant, futuristic court functioned so well was because it was SMALLER, considerably smaller. Here was a racquet sport that neutralized the serves. Serves did not dominate the game. Serves had to be spun into a smaller Soval (service-oval) to begin the point. Yet, the Soval was an OUT-area during the point. This was how you played singles on a court without lines. Servers understood that

~13~

the Soval (painted the same as the OUT-area around the court) was IN only on the serve, but was OUT during the point.

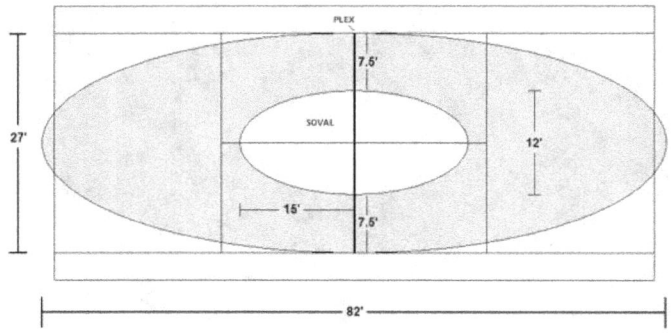

The net was not cloth. It was a soft but solid piece of something that resembled white Plexiglas (hemp). It was straight along the top instead of the usual bow of a net. No one got hurt if you ran into the "plex." They were easily replaceable if damaged. Streamline Scoring, like double-or-nothing, was a fascinating new way to score. Stadias were always packed to capacity when famous and very talented players took the courts.

A tabletop version of Roval was played by many citizens in their dome homes. It had the silly name of "Ring-Rong" and no one knew exactly why. There was also professional Ring-Rong played in smaller stadias. Ring-Rong balls bounced high and often hit the edges because there were more edges. The sport was cherished by many people and players, especially children.

Ring-Rong

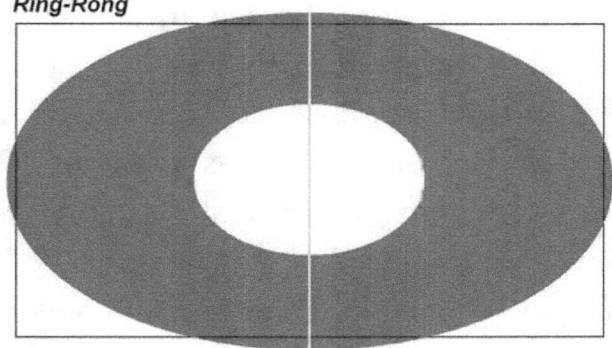

The game had a literal *hole* in the middle of the table with smooth, curved edges. Again, a smaller field (than what some citizens had in their distant memories) worked wonders and created a great game. A small plex divided the table.

Another game that most citizens had under their domes was called "R-Pool." Pocket pool or billiards that was *round* and only had one hole or pocket (void). Experts at R-Pool found it difficult to sink balls in this game. Different colored balls (same combinations as R-Games Chess) had to be sunk a certain way. It was not easy for great players to run the table as it was in a rectangular-shaped table.

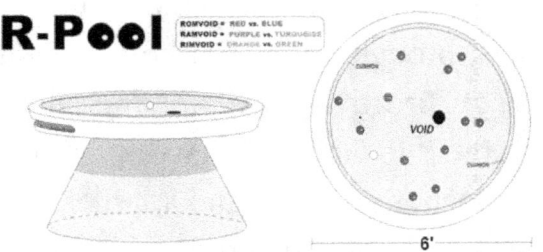

3 games can be played: red/blue balls must be CUT in.
Purple/turquoise balls must be hit in by combinations.
Orange/green balls must be banked in the hole [void].

More sports were popular activities among citizens, such as an Antigravity Basketball game called "Slammer," which was crazy to see. Players basically *flew* toward the basket. "Flog" was a type of golf where superballs were struck by special racquets that could travel up to an eighth of a mile in distance. You hit toward the goal which was a pin (4-inch hole) on a blue, not a green. Flog blues were composed of natural hemp and were very smooth. A smaller "flogger" (racquet) was for putts. The other major sport was a Dodgeball-type game called "Soccerball." There were "goalies" that guarded goals on either ends of a small field. Players had to be a certain distance away from the goals and players before they threw dodgeballs at them. People really enjoyed Soccerball because players were slowly eliminated and final actions were by only a few players. Media broadcast all sporting games and special contests were put on Mega Media channels so lifeforms off-world also viewed the events.

Arguably, the most exciting sport was not a physical activity. Romvoid, the bishop game, Ramvoid, the rook game and Rimvoid, the knight game, could be the most watched games throughout the Darkmoor Galaxy. It was intellect, strategy, creativity and thinking-ahead that were measured in the "R-Games." Two playing pieces: a small, solid cabochon or dome and a larger dome or bowl that was clear and lightly tinted a color. In the red/blue game of Romvoid, there was a row of pawns and the larger domes were all bishops. In one move, players could cover the pawn (Void) with a bishop (Rom) and the combination created a Queen! There was no King. In another move you could disengage the Queen and return to two separate pieces.

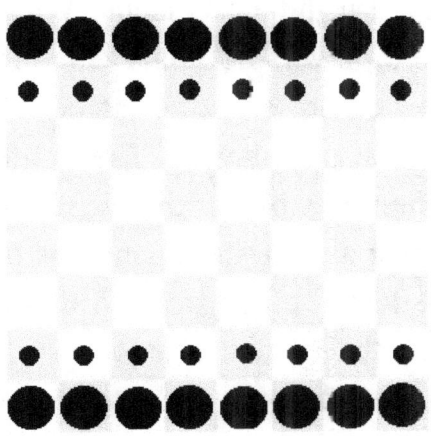

The action was incredibly fast in this board game that caught a large part of the galaxy's attention. *Multiple Queens attacked!* Lifeforms cheered, agonized, celebrated the different colored R-Games - they needed this type of cerebral brainwork after all the hardships they had experienced. The three R-Games were played in massive Stadiums. It was highly debated which game was the best or the one that was the most exciting.

Ramvoid had the prettiest colors, Purple vs. Turquoise, but might have been the least popular because it was based on rooks (castles). Rams moved along the rows, which was considered a "blunt" kind of game compared to how Roms moved along the diagonals.

Oddly, it was Rimvoid with the uninteresting colors of Green and Orange that was thought of as the most amazing R-game. Rims moved as knights in chess. Expert analysts loved this game because many Queens and Knights were on the board. And knights (Rims) were specially designed to attack Queens. Why were some of the best Romvoid players not that skilled in the other two R-games? You could say the same about the best Ramvoid and Rimvoid players. The contests were very specialized. Comments by pundits were everywhere over Mega Media when a top tournament was broadcast. Even the most sophisticated elites stopped important affairs of State and turned their attention toward Ceana whenever big contests happened.

Television provided remote super-HD pictures of every planet, all 13. Can you imagine? "Let's see the sunset on Venus tonight, dear." "Look, the Phobos obelisk has moved?!" "This has to be the best view of the rings." "Attack ships on fire off the shoulder of Orion." "There's C-beams glittering in the dark near Tannhauser Gate." ~*Just Imagine* what television could be<.

Also on Tele-Screens, citizens accessed incredible, super-drone views of Ceana's fantastic terrain (mountains, islands, seas, lakes, rivers, waterfalls, etc.). There were no commercials because there were no companies that profited. No capitalism. There was no money. There was no need for money. Free music and movies and other arts and entertainment were created by Masters that were simply out-of-this-world~.

Human life had been a wonderful experience on Ceana that had lasted for 10 centuries. People, in almost every case, lived extended lives and comfortably died in their sleep. The youth of present-day Ceana were the start of the 10th generation.

Once in a while, you would see *aliens*. Nothing bizarre or really creepy. They might have 3 eyes or 6 fingers or 3 boobs. You might have to get used to your neighbor with the antenna or blue skin. Maybe purple. But they were always good "people."

Those Watchers who observed Ceana in the larger sense, knew the factors that created its Millennium of Peace: If people were educated, trained well, had plenty to eat, had no countries, were not slaves to Money Systems, and actually had FUN and PLAYED with useful and extraordinary lives...

There would be peace. Human beings would live...beautifully...as they were meant to. Jefferson Blain believed people should not have to get up and go to *work* everyday. He believed people should get up and go to PLAY everyday. His subconscious mind designed Ceana so that society had daily fun and the minds of the masses were filled with extraordinary things. This was why fears, hatred, violence, killing and wars were totally alien to the citizens of Ceana (in the beginning).

***

Generations of Blains happened on the New Earth. Remember, there were two different Jeff Blains [like in the previous episode]: 1) JB who lived a happy dream life on Catalina with his wife, Teri. And...2) another real JB who has been kept in a comatose state aboard what was left of the Archon Science Ship, now the Moon. The parallel or connection with some assistance created Ceana. Whatever Jeff Blain conjured in his subconscious mind on the Rose for a thousand years, became reality on the planet with an 8000-mile diameter. He thought of himself and Teri on Catalina in a futuristic house with one very large, round window. They had two children, a boy and a girl...

That was a thousand years ago. Today on Ceana, the original 20,000 inhabitants had been gone for ages. The Creator, the designer, Jeff Blain, and his first families, were also long dead. But the Dreamer still dreamed and there remained just a bit more Angel Stardust to keep the Rose powered for a little longer. And when the power runs out as it will soon, what will happen then?

2 No More Angel Stardust

An eclipse occurred on Ceana between the yellow Sun and the Rose Moon with life on its surface. The astronomical event mystified astronomers because it was not supposed to happen, but it happened anyway. There weren't a lot of mysteries in the world. Scientists had a handle on most things and the intelligence level of the general public was very high. Did the Moon's orbit or the Sun's orbit or Ceana's orbit change? No. Instruments all recorded that there had been no variations in space. Normal rhythms should have occurred which never caused a solar eclipse previously. Why now and how could it have been possible?

Citizens were not fearful as ancient societies were of comets, eclipses and 'shooting stars.' They knew precisely why the Sun had been blocked and their reactions were not to panic or be fearful. They *wondered* about the unique event of the first time ever that their Sun had been eclipsed. Darkness in the Day. But they did not worry about it and were made to not worry about it over the planet's Media. The "best minds" at the time stated that: "The event was part of normal cycles of change whereby the Sun will be eclipsed in regular cycles from now on." Public statements were accepted as true. The truth was: No one was really certain how this happened or if it would ever happen again. Top authorities were worried, but did not let their real feelings out to the masses. The eclipse started a covert precedent unheard of before: The public will no longer receive the full Truth. Public statements would be guarded, curbed, even censored as not to cause panic among the citizenry. Very few people realized that their Free Society had turned into a Controlled Society.

***

Two (empty) Archon ziggurats remained and one was piloted by the Heart Center. The other Z-vehicles were all blasted to smithereens. He called a meeting with the Hope and she soon beamed in and materialized on the bridge of the Archon ziggurat. There was a lot to *talk* about. They spoke psychically:

Very good to see you again, Hope. They clasped hands. Her long, white hair moved from one side to the other. She looked up into his bright eyes. The Heart appeared older and still resembled a particular tennis player. *Do you understand how incredible it was for us to be spared? Of all our people, it was you...Our Hope that survived. I find it miraculous.* He smiled and showed facial wrinkles of a long life.

She did not match his happiness and let go. Her mind expressed doubts and fears with the thoughts: *I cannot hide my concerns. Sorry, if I forgo the formalities...*

Then tell me what are your hidden worries, dear?

Hope transmitted: *All this time we have been overseers of a small galaxy. They call it Darkmoor. Yes, there has been progress, great strides, amazing developments out of the Crisis and so much help from numerous Care Agencies....*

What is it? the Center asked.

The future. That is what I am afraid of, my Heart. What will happen next?

What do you see? Heart Center valued her insights and future projections more than any other Ranger or friend. He trusted her views more than any kind of Time Window or portal into Tomorrow.

I am seeing...Nothing. She turned away and expressed, *I fear our brothers and sisters did not transcend, did not pass through the White Gates and never reached the hallowed Halls of Elaraa.*

He saw it in her eyes; her thoughts came from her heart. He argued: *How can you believe that? You are not being...very...hopeful.*

Hope turned back and faced him. She answered and nearly laughed: *Eh, it is as if the Inversion never stopped and we have been thrown into the Mirror.* She got more emotional and serious. *From here, there is no transcendence. No Next Level. I have larger concerns than what will happen at the end of our lives...*

Tell me...

She replied, *I sense, see and feel a dark presence. You know who I mean?*

The Center responded: *Yes. Of all of our others, **he** had to be the one that lived. My double, the worst one. I can only sense he is alone in his empty Z-craft. We cannot locate the ship...*

We will, Hope added because she knew for certain that they would.

I am aware of his capture. But as you can also see, everything will not be as it appears. He will come to us with clean hands and surrender...

Hope finished Heart Center's thought: *...And we will not know his intentions, what the Dark One truly plans. He is...*

They searched for the best thought and only expressed: *Powerful.*

After a quiet/still moment, he asked, *Can you see and tell me any more of what will happen, Hope?*

She replied, *My Heart, I can feel the coming Darkness. Yes, once again. It will take the form of strangers, strange isos...but, it will also be another thing or many things that I cannot clearly resolve...*

Can you describe it?

Hope shook her head and her next word was very unspecific: *Dark.*

***

It was an odd afternoon, one fine day within Area 122, Zone 36, District 9, Territory 4. It shouldn't have been odd, but it was. Something did not seem quite right as if the air contained waves of doubt, suspicion and worry. Citizens felt a bit uneasy and uncertain, which were new emotions to a society that knew *it had nothing to fear.*

Whatever the electrical static or magnetism or frequency that felt *off* was, it only radiated out from this particular Area. Every other part of the globe carried on as usual - happy people who enjoyed their precious lives.

Three friends entered a sky-vehicle tower like they had done numerous times before. There was a Pikachu Head on the tower, but no one knew the character; it was merely a bright, funny face. Today, the boys decided to utilize the capsule's protective bubble and explore "Arz," the tallest and most beautiful mountain peak on Ceana (formerly, Mt. Everest). When they entered the tower, the three friends discovered that they were completely alone.

This was bizarre because the tower had been open to the public for hours and usually there were dozens or even a hundred citizens cued on different levels. They had the whole place to themselves. They thought, *Did no one in the area want to travel today?* Very odd.

The whole tower was automated and the trio understood how to move the "car" they chose to the top of the stack so that it could be ejected first. They also knew how to pilot the craft once operational and had no need for a bus driver. They decided on a 9-seater, which would have all three of them in the front 3 seats and they'd be 6 empty seats behind them. They punched in the Ain system for music and heard one of their favorite bands: "Facade." The sounds did not soothe them this time. They felt anxious about the whole trip. They weirdly turned the music off. *Should we do this?*

"Maybe there's something wrong with the tower?"

"Yeah, but the system would tell us that if it were true? Right?"

"Let's just take off."

"Okay. Let's go."

The boys saw that the power gauge was loaded to full capacity. Final buttons were pushed and *out like a rocket jettisoned the capsule!* When the sky-vehicle settled down after its initial thrust out of the Pikachu tower, the guys were not enjoying themselves like they usually did. The view was tremendous, spectacular! *Why did all three of them feel dread?* They could not get away from a sense of tension, first felt when they entered Area 122. *Had they carried some dark spectre with them?*

The boy in the middle turned around and looked behind him. He reacted emotionally and shouted in great fear to his friends: *"Hey! What's that!?"* The other two turned and observed...

Three men in the back row had on black suit jackets, white shirts, long ties, something on their heads and there was dark around their eyes. [The boys never saw such attire since suits, ties, hats and glasses did not exist on Ceana].

As the capsule passed over what was the south of France...*it disappeared.*

Three hours later, the same sky-vehicle materialized high over the south of France as a UFO. There were now 6 passengers onboard and they all resembled the first three strangers...

The A.I.N. System was about to broadcast to all Media agencies the news, *the strange disappearance of hover-capsule #8183121389 and its three passengers. The global system was countermanded.* The "perfect" system did not release the news to the public. Or the fact that more than one mysterious "iso" had invaded their *protected* world.

***

The Heart Center and the Hope remained together and were now located in the very center of the Moon. In other words, they were alone and onboard the Science Ship Rose. They were at the center of the place where Jeff Blain laid. The Teran continued his dream that had been woven out of Angel Stardust over the last one thousand years. Jefferson was alive, but not for long. The Great Ship, once home of countless Aliens and Archons, will be *dead* soon. And so will Jeff Blain.

The Center communicated to Hope: *Ha, he still looks good. We have used the man far too much...*

It was necessary, she added.

He must rest. He should be happy and not alone.

He will, soon.

Ceana

Hope. Can you feel it?

You mean the cold, the level of electricity? Warmth is almost gone, my Heart.

Not yet. Jeff still lives...a little while longer. Same with us, dear. Hold on a little while longer.

She gazed up into his sad and weary eyes. Hope expressed, *We have been invaded by isos, a growing cancer...*

The Darkness you expressed, once again. Yes.

Your other, the Dark Heart Center...he is defeated, yes? He is alone, is he not? How can he be responsible for the invasion? That world is protected from Negativity.

It was protected from Negativity. I can only assume he had help from Above. Or. More like assistance from down Below. What do you see of Darkmoor's overpopulation problem?

I see a resolution. A way is coming to quantum leap Planet-Building, the Hope told the Heart Center.

There is good news, then! Well, I am pleased to know that the galaxy will find relief. Then the former Archon leader got serious: *But what of Ceana?*

When power is gone, it will be gone forever, my love. That world was not established to be powered by real electrical methods, she sadly informed him.

No electricity. No power for homes. Nothing mechanical will function. How can we help Ceanan citizens, Hope?

We cannot even help ourselves. We are weak. We will all be gone soon. Remember. I saw nothing.

Both former (dying) gods stared down at the prone Jefferson Blain. They were of one mind and examined the "specimen" closely, his entire exterior, skin and peaceful face.

On the subject of Jeff, Heart Center relayed the thought: *Lucky bastard~.*

Hope laughed. *Ha, ha, now why would you express that to me?*

He replied, *Because I think I know what will happen to him...*

***

Along with your occasional alien with blue, green, purple or yellow skin, there were now odd characters in society that wore black. [Black had been the one color 100% omitted or avoided in clothing/fashions on Ceana]. Head-pieces or head-dresses (Earth fedoras) were worn on their heads and no one had ever done that. It was as if these pale-skinned humanoids were just another uniformed band of aliens that landed on the planet and took up residence. They were known as the "Monitors."

They did not speak. No one spoke to them. They were left alone.

The A.I.N. System declared them: "mostly harmless." It recommended that citizens should steer clear of these *potentially dangerous aliens*. No incidents were viewed or recorded to the masses. Robo-police units monitored the Monitors and stood ready to act to protect the public if the need arose.

Mega Media announced what top officials of Territories had reported: In outer space, a monumental Event had occurred and citizens throughout the systems of Darkmoor were informed: *Their old Enemy, the Dark Lord and leader of the Narchons, had been captured!* A large majority of galactic survivors thought their Enemies, those who started the War on this level, were completely destroyed. And it was the counter to Heart Center (the worst one) that lived? The thought was *unsettling*, but citizens were collectively satisfied to know that the horned Demon was found and imprisoned.

Mega Media outlets did not inform solar systems that the *Dark Lord surrendered peacefully*. No, the accepted story was "a mighty battle in space occurred between the Robot-Army and Dark Heart's ziggurat," which resulted in many casualties of operators. The Demon was apprehended after a dramatic exchange of weapon-fire. Films of the historic event were released to those on Mega Media galactic channels. The big news story and film footage were totally faked.

***

Citizens born on Ceana were not given names at birth. At the age of one, children talked fluently and named themselves. A lot of decisions were given to children who did not take advantage of their liberties. Parents respected children and children respected parents. Everyone was smart, well-guided and basically very well-behaved. One particular citizen named herself: "Jain." She was a 10th generation, direct descendant of Jeff Blain and Teri Howard, but she wasn't aware of that fact. She was a bit different than most girls. She had "spider-senses." Outside of aliens on Ceana, every citizen chose a name of one word. Surnames were not used.

Jain was a loner with long, yellow hair. She never married and there were marriages on the planet. Most did not. She kept a family residence on Catalina although the land and structures had drastically changed in a millennium. Her clear, spherical home was located on the edge of the Pax (Pacific) Ocean, very near the shoreline. At high tide, the clear sphere looked as if it floated on the waves. This part of the island had chlorophyll tinted blue so visitors never saw green plants. They'd be blue.

The girl enjoyed her occupation. (Some citizens worked in fields of Service. They were self-motivated and *wanted* to do these necessary jobs). She loved mysteries and worked as a modern detective. She was psychic for a human and took on cases from people who needed help and knew she had special skills.

At the moment, she was on a case. A husband and wife had walked into her office and reported their missing son. He'd been missing for weeks along with two of his good friends. They told Jain that magistrates said there were no records that her son and the two other boys *had even existed.* The Head Magistrate told them or threatened all the parents that if they pursued the matter any further, they would be considered *insane* and be "removed from society for public safety reasons." The story of the missing boys touched Jain's heart and she took the case. She believed them. But, there were no leads. How could she solve the case and bring some closure to the distraught parents?

She used her senses and asked the Universe to help her. And it did. Jain saw few stars above and the famous (new) constellations of 'Avater,' 'Borg' and 'Longenis.' The answer or lead was received and that thought was: "iso." Creatures that should never have appeared and thrived in the matrix (society), but there they were. Not your usual type of extraterrestrial. Unplanned, unseen, pale, mute humanoids that hated the light and wore dark glasses to protect their large black eyes. Even the diffused light of Ceana's Sun was too much for these "creeps." They also stayed away from water for some odd (electrical) reason. Jain sensed there was a connection to the Higher Floor above their level of Life. Were the Super Giants Upstairs behind the black invasion? Had the Super Gods always been secret Puppet-Masters for us on the lower level? Yes, somehow these Men in Black were connected to the recent changes in the world and also connected to the recently "captured" Dark Heart Center. Jain just knew it and saw the truth in mind-pictures.

She hid near one of the weird dwellings where the Monitors "lived." It was a secluded community shielded with legal forcefields. Jain was right at the edge of the barrier and went to lightly touch it...

The young lady in a grey jumpsuit with mini-equipment was instantly *beamed through the forcefield wall and into a silent den of dark demons...*

><

Jain remained cool and steady as she was surrounded by 7 of these creeps. Of course, the round room was very dark. The girl saw black curtains in the background. When the curtains moved, she noticed small lights on alien machines. She was afraid, but she controlled her fears and approached the situation with confidence.

"Listen, buddies! I don't know what's going on here. Monitors, huh? Well, take a good look! What do you see?!" The girl clenched her fist, gathered up extra energy, pumped her fist and took two steps toward them. *What would these fuckers do?* was her thought.

Two in front of her stepped back.

"Ha." This told her a few things: They weren't that strong and powerful at all; they were just creeps! Jain's overconfidence did not last long.

The Men in Black in ties and fedoras grabbed her! She fought them and got a few good licks in until they all jumped her at one time. Jain could not reach for a repellant spray on her belt because they had her arms pinned back. Suddenly, *they bit her!*

"Fuck! Stop with the biting!!"

They bit her in the legs and on one of her breasts. Their teeth were sharp. The jumpsuit was torn and she bled. Jain took deep breaths and was able to kick them enough to be released from their grasp.

At that moment, another of the creatures entered the scene from between the curtains and psychically shouted to his 7 comrades: *STOP!* And they stopped the attack on the girl. This one appeared very similar. He or it waved a pale finger in front of the others: *No, children.* They left the room. Then he turned to Jain and expressed: *They are young, they are new, they will learn. They are your kind and must be trained...*

Jain was in pain and asked the Vampire, "How are

you different from them?"

I thought you were a good observer? He pointed to the single medallion pinned to his black jacket. *They wore no single stripe. I do.*

"Whatever the hell that means? Ugh. Now what?"

The Monitor replied in a calm manner: *Now we fix you. This will not happen again. By the way, we brought you here. We need your services, Jain...*

"Really?" She heard every psi-thought from the creature as clear as a bell.

***

The Hope died. The Heart Center was with her when she passed and disappeared. For all the knowledge contained within the former leader of the gods, he was uncertain if she walked through the White Gates and entered Elaraa Heaven. He was the last Archon, except for his evil twin brother. The Heart cried.

3 Death of Jeff Blain

Mega Media was tuned in everyday by lifeforms on extremely populated planets that were desperate to be relocated to newly manufactured planets, moons and stations. They waited and waited for the next available space in space. Recent efforts to increase production failed. A few artificial planets had collapsed in on themselves because the building process was hurried to meet the needs of the galaxy. The results had been catastrophic, the loss of millions of lives!

Yet (with the death of the Hope) there was hope. Somehow when situations were at their worst, during a terrible crisis, a guiding light might come in and give warmth and comfort. And it happened. Many felt it: *The next attempt to solve the overpopulation problem will succeed.* Everyone had to hold on longer and be hopeful.

The next stage of things to come was an optimistic view of the future. It came in the form of the "World Generator." Ceanan State scientists devised an enormous Machine that tapped into the turning planet. Electrical Power could be made to *explode outwardly* and then the energy directed back to the planet and then finally be directed to any point on the surface of Ceana. The galaxy's problems were one thing, but few people on

Earth 2.0 knew that their electrical power [Angel Stardust] had dwindled for years. Horribly low. The Big News of an imminent global disaster was withheld from the public. Elite officials knew there were alternatives to avoid 'The Day Ceana Stood Still,' so why warn people of a possible disaster?

The World Generator was in its late planning stages. The public was told that the WG was the *new attempt to quicken Planet-Building.* The idea gained tremendous support by citizens and masses off-world. Everyone was for it, it was pushed and it was ratified by the highest elite officials. Ceana was one of the most protected planets in Darkmoor (true) and that was the prime reason for the Power Station's construction on a "special planet blessed by the gods." Ceana = God is Merciful.

Construction had begun on the Largest of Machines that made the whole planet a World Generator or Power Broadcaster to the rest of the galaxy. The project would not be completed for years. WG campaigns lied. There was no way, initially, that the WG Phase I could ever broadcast power to be utilized on other star systems. Head Magistrate and only a few of the best scientists were aware of this fact. The withheld truth was: *The Generator would only be used to supply electrical power to Ceana.* When the Energy of dead Archons vanished to nothing...the machines, the industries, the devices, all communications systems, every channel of Media, will not CRASH. Ceanan Society should continue without a hitch, without interruption. Instead of power levels that drained to nothing, the Energy Tanks will be *recharged* and everything will continue as it was. The future "Power Planet" must be stabilized first. [Media networks broadcast only the partial truth. Forecasts of 'bad news' were withheld from the public].

***

One of the Sky-Capsules, a large one with a hundred passengers, fell out of the sky when it was only 30 feet over Lake Lindalore. It plunged into the water. Citizens of Ceana were the best swimmers and the passengers swam to shore. No one was seriously hurt. But why did the incident happen? Media reports stated that it was "a simple malfunction." The truth was: A power drain zapped the local electrical energy because global levels were so depleted. The aircraft did not have the hover-power as it should have had. An emergency crisis situation was in place, but the general public had no clue. They only knew that "temporarily" all flight towers were closed until the capsule systems were made safe again. State officials were extremely lucky that there were no fatalities from higher vehicles that flew on low tanks.

Similar occurrences happened on the seas and lakes. Small boats to luxury liners were stranded. Pilots and drivers believed they had enough energy in the tank and they were suddenly wrong. All passengers were rescued.

The power losses had become an epidemic. Media downplayed (ignored) hundreds of strange energy drains while the AIN only reported a few.

There were large arrays of artificial satellites that orbited Ceana. These were mostly AIN Systems that had to do with programming the weather, making snow wherever it was ordered, physical teleportation (beaming) of products and supplies, air filtration and conditioning, "monitoring" every square inch of the planet closely for entertainment purposes as well as security. Satellite systems decided (could decipher) if incoming spacecrafts were hostile or not. A Negativity-Meter calculated the results and if lifeforms possessed strong negative auras, a soft barrier prevented them from landing. If the isos had entered Ceana from space, they would have been turned away. That was not how they arrived into this world.

(In the area of what was Switzerland a long time ago) Ceanan citizens walked along a safe, electric-bridge between mountains. The artificial walkway was over three miles long and *invisible* to the eyes! Visitors appeared to have "walked on air" and were surrounded by bright, colorful, majestic, mountain peaks and valleys. Everything was very beautiful and supremely perfect, until it wasn't anymore:

THE ELECTRIC BRIDGE or thin/extended forcefield, inexplicably shut OFF!

3200 citizens and a few aliens perished that day!
There had never been a mechanical failure that caused even one fatality in the past. The loss was felt all over the planet and for lightyears beyond. *WHY?* was the question. State authorities could not cover up the horrible tragedy at "Rainbow Bridge." People came together and mourned the dead in a number of Media affairs and presentations. Families of the unfortunate ones were never the same. "Deaths at Rainbow Bridge would never be forgotten," various channels declared. The whole planet and beyond felt the pain. The truth, to a great degree, had to go public this time: A power failure, obviously. Similar situations had occurred in every Territory and District. It was all connected to the "malfunctions" and why Flight Towers and other public services were ON HOLD.

Also, there were times that food dispensers *stopped!* The low energy crisis struck every dome home at that point. Food tablets and capsules were stuck in the machines and could not be removed. With an entire/global food-system that relied on fully functional dispensers, *there was mass panic!* Also, no new food was produced>.

Citizens now realized they were in big trouble and some of them *feared* for the first time in their lives. Relief for Ceana was on the horizon, truly. [?] The World Generator was not completed, but some electrical power could be siphoned off to aid the crisis on Ceana. And it was...

Soon, Flight Towers, boat rides, stadias, personal devices, dispensers, the underground system, etc. will be online. ["The Games will begin again!"]. As promised by State magistrates, electrical levels increased and were scientifically shown to the public that they had been increased. More *juice* was coming with a Generator that enlarged with more power every minute. Once this fact was proven to citizens, fears went away. Trust and confidence in the AIN systems were renewed. In time, most buildings and machines and conveniences were back to normal. *Thank the Makers!*

***

Within the weird/irregularly-shaped and very dark dwelling of the Monitors, Jain and the main Monitor moved to another portion of the place. Previously, she had walked through a machine that instantly healed her wounds. Her grey jumpsuit was replicated like new by another machine. The *brightly-lit,* empty room was completely unexpected to her. It contained two things that resembled chairs...

"What?" Jain was astounded because she felt and assumed these suited creeps with hats could not take bright lights. "Now you guys like the light?" Both of them sat.

No, Detective. Things are not as they seem. The pale creature smiled and showed his sharp teeth. He took off his fedora that covered a bald head. He also removed his dark glasses and revealed the large, black eyes of the iso alien. *Who am I?*

Jain was stunned and thought: *This fellow sure was different.* She repeated his thought-question, "Who are you? Oh, this is some kind of test, is it? I'm good at tests. I have no problem understanding your thoughts..."

Concentrate. Let's see how good you are, eh? I'm going to implant a certain personage into your brain, that person is who I am, under this skin, understand? I'm sending now. Who am I?" The Monitor's hand held his chin and his big black eyes glared at her.

The girl definitely received an image and that terrible image had horns. "You're the fucking last Narchon. The Horned Beast, or should I just call you Dark Heart Center?"

You are good, ha, ha, ha.

"Explain to me, if that were true, what is the thing that the Robot Army has imprisoned at Tannhauser Gate?"

Ha, ha. 'E's an awfully quiet sort of chap, aye? And have you noticed he doesn't like light and stays in the dark?

"Now, I get it. He's the creep and you're the Black Center."

Bravo. Two stars, go to the head of the class, dear. I knew you'd get it.

"You can exchange places with the Monitors anytime you want, I take it?

This one, anyway. They didn't summon you here, I did...

"Why? You said you have need for my services. What the hell do you want me to do, oh, Evil One? Like I would trust your words, huh?"

Well, what if I told you and the world the plain truth? Nothing but the truth? I swear to me.

"Be more specific. What's the plan? What do you intend on doing and how does that include me?"

An exclusive interview, you'll interview me to Mega Media...

"Ha, uh." She choked and almost gagged for some reason. After a swallow, Jain expressed to the demon vampire: "Mega Media, to all of Darkmoor? Seriously?"

Why not? His whitish face appeared puzzled. *I'll put it to you this way, sweetie: Don't know if you've heard, but interrogations with me, I mean my minion, ain't going too well and won't be. His conscious mind is mush;*

he's waiting for orders and there are none coming. The Head Magistrate has a proposal to execute the Narchon leader, a galactic Event, my Death...and it will happen. We only have a short time.

"Wait. Okay? Let's say the thing that looks like you is put to death...?"

Then I die too.

"I'm not certain of that."

It's why we should hurry. I have a lot to say. Everyone in Darkmoor wants to hear from the Narchon. Well, they'll get nothing from that automaton at Tannhauser Gate. I'm the one you want to question. They want the Dark Heart Center to pay for his Crimes against Life. If they rub my stooge out...I still live. What do you have to say to that, Jain?

"Sure, I could present your story, whatever's true? I work with lab people, scientists, who know the Higher-Ups. You'd have to be tested. *Both*, you and your minion with Deep Diagnostic machines, mind-probe machines, to get to the bottom of this. Let the top brass decide who's who, or maybe they'll just fry both your ugly asses, you know, to make sure? What about this interview? You want to make a final statement? Confession? A few regrets, maybe, like NOT starting the Great War?!"

Suddenly, she sensed the Monitor shell and the Narchon soul absolutely had become 100% sincere [or was he?] when he spoke aloud in English to her with the words: "You can ask any question you'd like about the past and I'd do my best to respond. But, I think Darkmoor's survivors are far more interested in what is to come. Yes, in my statement to the world, I want to tell them the pure truth of what is happening now and exactly what will happen in the future. Overpopulation situation. This is what is imperative. They must hear what I have to say. By speaking truly of this new Generator and the growing Phantom Menace that very few World Citizens are aware of, then possibly, another galactic Disaster could be averted. I want to clear..."

"Stop! Please. Save your speeches for the interview, eh? What do I call you? You need a name if we're going to do this? Yes?"

"It *would* be odd for you to refer to me as Dark Heart when I look like this." The creature smiled a big smile and revealed his pointed teeth. "How about 'Stripe' because the original Monitors only have one stripe on their jacket?" He pointed to his chest.

"Stripe, it is."

"You know you'll be famous because of this?" Stripe commented.

"I don't care about that," she replied with a serious

expression on her face. "I'm curious what you have to say."

***

Heart Center was alone and sat on the highest peak of his favorite crater on the Moon, Arzachel. It was where he meditated and relaxed: atop the high center mountain peak. The Archon looked down and observed the large, inner crater he called "Eden." He wondered if this was the last time he'd see such wondrous sights? Tears were in his glassy eyes. The clean air felt cool on his skin. There was a slight breeze. He took large breathes and he rubbed his hairless face.

One of the colonies (Escher) had occupied his crater for the last 200 years. He didn't mind. They did not know it was his private *home*, the one place he cherished in the entire (replicated) solar system. Well, the thin/central mountain, anyway (Shera Pree). And it was the real one in the other world, but this real one would do. He often flew to the top and made himself invisible when he wanted to get away and be alone. Hardly anyone from the colony ever ventured up to the high point. Old Heart thought that was very strange. Good for him because he adored solitude and not having the weight of the galaxy lay on his shoulders. His decisions. He wanted rest. He thought about the Halls of Elaraa and what they would look like. His long life would soon end. He wondered: If he died, would his twin die? If his twin died, would he die? In a short time, he would know.

He said aloud, as if he spoke to the Hope, "You were wrong, my love. It won't work. The Big Relief for the galaxy, the Great Plan for Reconstruction, the *Quantum Leap* you expressed to me. Generator II, the Second Phase, will not work and will be the End of Everything! Exactly what you transmitted to me...the final End Game will result in...Nothing..."

The Heart Center found a horizontal place among the soft, blue rocks and he laid on it. He closed his eyes. After a few more heavy breathes, he fell into a deep meditative state where he Astral Projected...

***

Jain was in one of those labs she knew of with one of her very close friends, Dorsey. Dorsey had her own laboratory and worked with the robo-police. She was also a big Media geek and knew everything about AIN computers. [Computers on Ceana worked and never came with viruses, unlike certain computers 1000 years ago].

Jain told her friend everything, the whole experience with the Monitor she believed was the real Dark Heart or the spirit of the Dark One. The big interview would happen; State officials approved it. The scientists, an army of tech assistants and many armed guards stood at the ready. The subject with horns held at Tannhauser and the Monitor who called itself 'Stripe' would both be examined carefully. Side by side. After intense study by the best psychic minds, technicians and quality machines, a decision would be rendered. The Head Magistrate will make the final call.

Jain audio-recorded the conversation with the Monitor without his knowledge. Or maybe with his knowledge? When her grey suit was replicated, all of her mini-equipment was also recreated. She merely turned on the recorder...

"...It would be odd for you to refer to me as Dark Heart when I look like this. How about 'Stripe' because the original Monitors only have one stripe on their jacket?"

"Stripe, it is."

"You know you'll be famous because of this?"

"I don't care about that...I'm curious what you have to say."

Jain turned off the recorder and said to Dorsey: "That wasn't the important part."

The redhead said, "There wasn't much on the tape, Jain."

Jain replied, "There was more. Before that was all in my head, not on tape."

Dorsey said, "I don't know how convincing an audio or even an interview would be. Unless they could match speech patterns. Do they have recorded words by the Narchon leader?"

Jain replied, "Probably not. They wouldn't need it..."

Dorsey responded: "Huh?"

"We have words of our dear Heart. I've actually met him once. Take his words, reverse them, see if there was a connection or harmonic parallel, something that would connect with the talking Monitor?"

"You met him? I have to hear more about that." Then Dorsey offered, "But what will decide where the Dark One is, which one he is, will be the battery of tests that will be put to both of them. I can help with the necessary personal. What will happen after that with the authorities, who the hell knows, eh? Great seeing you again, Jain. We should go out and do something together, sometime? Whenever we can break free, that is." The cute girl rolled her green eyes and smiled.

"Great. We'll do that, Dor." She smiled back. "I knew I could count on you." Jain kissed Dorsey on the lips and left the lab.

***

A titanic **EXPLOSION** occurred at a special "safety-valve" location along the Ceanan Power Grid!

The Valve was installed by the Heart Center. *This was the leader's personal and private Ziggurat.* One of two that survived the War. The other was his counterpart's Ziggurat, which was tossed into Ceana's Sun. For the longest time, the Electrical Pressure of the planet was released through Heart's Ziggurat and the system held to a crucial stability that did not change. Heart Center's plan was supposed to stop the Accelerator from any more accumulated Energy. Power would remain at a constant level. The Electric Power would continue to feed colonies on other star systems and also not damage Ceana any further. The plan failed when the Valve failed to contain the Super Energy that was run through the Grid. It **BLEW!** The last shred of hope was gone. Nothing could stop the inevitable destruction of "Jeff's Planet." In truth, the Great Explosion was the Death of the Heart Center. But he did not know it until later...

From the Moon's (Arzachel) peak, the Heart Center projected his consciousness to the side of Jefferson Blain's med-bed on the Rose, deep down inside the planet to its core. He stood up in his ethereal body and looked at the man. His hand touched the man's cheek. Jeff hadn't aged in all these years. The Center said, "Thank you, son. Thank you for everything. I wanted to be with you at this moment. So you wouldn't be alone. So *we* wouldn't be alone when we die...like tears in the rain."

The Heart Center and JDB died at the very same time<>. Center Heart had more work, more paths to travel and he only saw the Halls of Elaraa from a great distance. It existed, it truly existed, but heaven was a bit further up the Road.

The Dark Heart Center, the one in captivity and the creature at the Monitors' dwelling did not die. They were both alive and well, one mute and one who wanted to tell the world everything.

Did anything in the real world change because of Jeff's death? No. Nothing changed. Nothing changed. Why? Angel Stardust, the last trace of pixie dust (electricity) disintegrated to zero. It was all gone. There was no more Magic in the world. WHY did nothing change? Maybe because they utilized an electrical substitute, the World Generator, which gained more and more energy everyday!? But the generated power wasn't supposed to be adapted to Jeff's conjured and projected planet that operated differently. And yet, Ceana's AIN and wide spectrum of other systems were fully energized. Global power levels rose. It was not supposed to happen, but it happened.

The EM power on Ceana and throughout the rest of Darkmoor increased and increased and increased<. *The Energy was never going to stop its acceleration and accumulation!!* Very few living entities clearly viewed and understood what was going to happen in the future. Windows into Tomorrow were shattered, conflicted and were no longer reliable sources of knowledge. It was 'business as usual' on the Power Planet, for now. Hardly a soul noticed that society had taken a dark turn: There were terrible crimes, organized crimes, gangs, murders and the rumblings of all-out *War*. The 'face of Ceana,' once a utopia for a small number of citizens, will drastically change in the years ahead. The Creator, Designer, and Engineer, was dead.

TS Caladan

4 The Last Narchon

Completion ceremonies for the World Generator were broadcast over Mega Media! The huge, metal ARCH or circular structure that was the WG was two miles in height! It was a fantastic feat of engineering that was believed to "save us all."

There was other NEWS. Big news that stunned everyone that heard it, beyond opening ceremonies. It was broadcast that the "Great Generator saved Ceana and will do the same for the rest of Darkmoor." In time. There were joyous festivals and happiness on Jeff's planet. But the rest of the galaxy *still had to wait.* Lifeforms were told that new planet-building had increased production much more than before the Generator. That was not the case; it was another lie that citizens everywhere did not know. For the most part, lifeforms believed what was transmitted over Mega Media.

The [filtered, bittersweet] News was: The completed "Arch" was only Phase I, which proved the principle and Ceana was saved. *Phase II would do the same for the worlds of Darkmoor.* Planet production would increase by a factor of 100. Calculations told the team of Arch scientists that the galactic crisis would end in a Ceanan year because of large numbers of safe habitats that would be built at that time. Off-world worlds simply had to struggle to survive for a little while longer.

Everyone was informed by Mega Media that because of higher levels of power, more needed supplies will arrive and more vertical living-spaces will be constructed. [It was one more lie to zillions of lifeforms].

***

The High Magistrate, in his most splendid purple outfit, stared through the strongest of forcefields at the naked Horned Beast. *It so appeared like the Heart.* The Monster cowered in pain in a corner that had the dimmest light after the Magistrate had the Tannhauser operators hit the bright lights. The creature shook and covered his eyes.

"Do it again!" the top Official on Ceana loudly commanded.

The masked operator pushed the switch and bigger ceiling lights came on and the creature screamed in pain once more: "Aaaaaaaaugh!" The operator pushed the switch back and the big lights went off.

Magistrate yelled at the operator: "I didn't tell you to stop!"

The slave quickly hit the switch again and the Narchon screamed again. It screamed in horrible pain *continuously* as the lights remained on!

"That's better." Then he shouted amid terrible cries of pain: "Do you know how many citizens don't want your head and are against the broadcast execution?! No! They want *this* to happen to you, for you to burn every second for what you did!"

The operator who lost family in the Great War long ago thought this was too cruel of an act.

"Why won't you talk?! You have much to answer for, demon!" screamed the High Magistrate. "The torture will stop, answer our questions or just say *something!*"

The Horned Beast groveled on the floor of the prison cell in extreme pain. It said nothing. It could not say anything. It was a Monitor and not the last Narchon. "Aaaaaaaaaah!!"

The High Magistrate ordered the operator. "Hose him down. See if he likes that any better, eh?"

"Yes, sir."

***

Final preparations were completed. All was in place for one particular Monitor to speak to those anxious listeners and viewers over Mega Media. Humans and aliens were told the following 'Interview With A Monitor' may or may not be an interview with the Dark Heart Center. Viewers were totally aware of the situation, the possibility that this Monitor was not a Monitor. The anatomy of the alien creeps were known: They had no vocal chords. It would be impossible for one of the fedora fellows to talk. Audiences were informed the real news that the Monitor and the prisoner at Tannhauser would be intensely examined together on the largest Science satellite of Ceana known as 'Jericho Station.' Before that, the Monitor wanted to speak. And a world listened...

Jain sat in the same brightly-lit room that she was in before and a large squadron of Robo-Police lined the round walls. Lesser minion Monitors ("children") were not in the domicile. Right after the Mega Media interview, the talking Monitor would be shipped to Jericho Station along with the tortured Beast. Jain and Stripe sat on the sitting-devices and faced each other. The bald iso alien wore no sunglasses or fedora.

Jain started with the statement: "We will not know for sure what we are dealing with here until later, your claim that you are the real Narchon or spirit of Dark Heart Center. And what we have captured as the Beast is a Monitor, under the skin. The Beast is hurt by light; it screams but cannot speak: This supports your claim, *Stripe*, as you want to be called. The Out-of-Body phenomenon or soul transfer is an ancient technique and a well-established fact. *Is Soul Transfer the case here?* is the question. You have told me and officials that you have important information or a message you must relay to us. Tell me and the rest of the galaxy...why should we believe you?"

"Why, indeed? You shouldn't believe me, if I am who I say I am. I speak and should not be physically able to. Am I hypnotizing everyone? How is it possible? What will your scientists and psychics say at the end of their long and grueling tests on me and the other one? Your mind-probes and diagnostics will prove to everyone that my words are true..."

"Alright, let's assume your words are true, Dark Heart, and not Stripe. My question is WHY? Why inform us of the Truth? You said we should not believe you. Isn't it illogical or irrational for us to believe the words of the negative Center or Heart? It would be like believing the words of the antichrist, yes? Why? Why are your words 'imperative'? Why are you telling us this? What do you intend? What do you mean by telling us this message?"

Monitor shell and Narchon soul said: *"I only mean to speak the truth and for the systems of Darkmoor to do with the information, these insights of Things to Come, what you will with them. This is exactly what will happen. Your Fate cannot be avoided. Isos have miraculously appeared inside the Matrix. Isos are true creatures made from the Darkness. I only look like one on the outside. Why am I speaking? Not to clear my conscience. I am speaking because Dark Heart is also a Puppet of the Higher Super Gods on the next Level Above. So was the Heart. I have been ordered to do what I have done. Today...and a thousand years ago. We are all Monitor-Slaves, machines who obey and answer to higher masters. I am no different than you..."*

Jain expressed: "Interesting. Interesting that you take no responsibility for your actions and blame your GODS for all the destruction. It wasn't you, it was THEM who were behind everything, right? Alright. You said you want to deal with present situations and the future, rather than dwelling on the past. Please, the floor is yours. What is your message?"

He straightened his black tie and relaxed. Stripe told the world: *"It has to do with the World Generator, which will soon be turned into a Particle Accelerator and appear very different than the two-mile high Arch. It will assume the form of very tall power stations or terminals that irregularly circle the globe, towers of power, very BLACK in color. They will have uniform vents and very small green lights and the sound created will be a continuous hum. The planet will be encased within a continuous twilight. Ceana's electrical power will increase by a thousandfold! Mega Media will proclaim this to be your Savior, a successful answer to overpopulation by boosting Planet-Building in Quantum Leaps! They will refer to Ceana's Phase II by calling it a*

Ceana

'Positive Particle Accelerator.' It will succeed! For the longest time, 'natural' planets and satellites will be manufactured into existence relatively quickly and vast numbers of Life will migrate to these new worlds. Everything went divinely for ages...until it reached a tipping-point. The Accelerator continued accumulating Power, Power and more Power! Strange things started to appear or simply materialized on Ceana. Reality shattered like shards of a mirror. Especially around the Terminals that grew even taller. Creatures from other times and other dimensions and far away/alien worlds suddenly existed on the planet near the ominous Towers. Slowly, Ceana was poisoned by Phase II. High officials also called the Great Machine a Particle COLLIDER. What insiders knew but could do nothing about was...'Collider' really meant a Reality Collider! The Accelerator caused reality to rip apart in places, cracked seams, and those were the places where strange animals and weird machines started to appear in these openings around the black towers...

"Let me stop you there. You claim this will all occur in the future. To me, it does not matter what the technicians and other experts conclude about you at Jericho Station. The truth in your words could be determined by waiting and seeing if your prognostications or views of tomorrow will really happen on Ceana. Yes?"

Stripe/Dark Heart smiled and displayed his sharp teeth again. He reached his arms out a bit and showed the viewers his pale, empty hands. He nodded and said as he closed his big, black eyes for a moment: *"I am in your hands."*

Jain remembered and asked, "You also mentioned averting another galactic Doomsday? You haven't explained the problem. What will go wrong with upgraded, Phase II Planet-Building and what will be the end result?"

"After much time and much success, new planets and moons will not remain in their stable condition. They will bio-degrade, lose cohesion and crumble to dust in a short time after being fed more and more power continuously. This will happen virtually at once. There will be No Hope for those who thought they had moved to Paradise-Planets. Such great galactic losses happened so swiftly and utterly that there was no one left to rescue survivors like there had been before. Darkmoor got even darker and colder and soon everything just died. Like a candle that flickered, faded and was extinguished. In the end, there was...nothing."

"Stripe..." Jain felt the need to interject, terminate his train of thought for the large audience. "...Let's say your words were true and we start down this path that will lead to the end of everything. What can stop it?" She hoped there was optimism somewhere.

Ceana

"Nothing. Nothing can stop it. It can't be stopped! It's not supposed to be stopped. When new planets crumble, electrical-flux forces will be so intense at the source that Ceana will be torn apart. Ceana will be torn apart also~"

"Hold on. You stated or gave the impression you wanted to avert this coming mega Disaster. Now you say it's an inevitable fate and our Doom is sealed?! Which one is it, Dark Heart?"

Without hesitation, it replied: *"I also said your Fate cannot be avoided.* At first I thought there was Hope. But things have changed and now there is no hope for any of us..."

"Okay. That's enough." Jain gave a hand sign and the broadcast ended.

***

The very next day, the thing that resembled a Narchon was electrocuted with electricity boosted by the Wireless World Generator. Dead. Well-filmed, so the whole world observed it. The same was done with the creepy Monitor in a fedora that spoke. There were no tests run at Jericho Station. The High Magistrate decided that it did not matter what the scientists concluded on: Who was who? The entire affair needed to end and was terminated with the electrocutions broadcast on Mega Media.

***

Monitors on Ceana, the "children," were fast asleep. All of them. But one of them was not. It had 3 stripes on his jacket and it activated. He *woke*, he moved and he spoke: *"Ha. My next words...no one will ever hear. It was not any Higher Level Above or lower level below that instigated and will carry out the total destruction of Darkmoor...it was the one that I faithfully serve: Queen Zep."*

5 *Positive Particle Accelerator*

The first part of the talking Monitor's message came true. Two years later, the massive Arch (at what used to be New York City) was de-constructed. All two miles of it, piece by piece. In no way did this change power levels for Ceana or the Accelerated Levels of Super Electricity fed to the machines of off-world Planet-Building. Omni-Energy was totally contained and controlled. It was discovered that the Arch Source Generator *could be turned off for years* and still: Power flowed! Electrical Inertia. Phase II had begun. Most aware lifeforms of Darkmoor were not concerned or worried that the actions taken today were wrong and would lead to the end of everything. Few believed the words of the confined creep, words that faded into obscurity as time marched on. The situation was very different for State Insiders. They believed. Yet, there was no more World Generator. In the near future, there will only be the "Positive Particle Accelerator."

Precisely what Dark Heart Monitor declared with confidence came true. Phase II was better described as a *Particle Accelerator,* and a "Positive" one at that. Its new title served a vital purpose: It alleviated fears inside every human and alien under the 'umbrella' of its Power. *The global structure of Phase II would surely have a grand*

POSITIVE effect as it boosted electricity in every sense, everywhere. Life was assured: There would be no negative repercussions from the next stage of the Generator. It was safe. But, there will be "sacrifices" for citizens of Ceana, for the good of the rest of the galaxy. In the beginning of this new era, citizens were comforted by State authorities when they said that the Power would be "contained, controlled and used wisely."

More of the Monitor's predictions were right on the mark, apparently. Very large, black circles started to appear in an odd global pattern across the planet. Citizens did not know and were not informed (exactly) what they were. It was accepted that the dark circles were part of Phase II. Quickly, the Spots grew. Not larger in circumference, taller. Worldwide Spots grew vertically. In time, citizens saw there was another level or floor on top of the circles. No machines or people constructed the Positive Particle Accelerator. It was as if the entire network was built by "invisible hands." The Great Arch was physically constructed and deconstructed, but Phase II almost appeared by Magic.

Day by day, the structures extended more and more. Higher and higher. Another level and another level of BLACKNESS. They almost resembled reverse Stadias, back when there used to be Games on the planet, except for their color. Anyone who came near the spooky structures heard an unmistakable HUM in the air around them. The air was dense, cloudy and electrified. Citizens were in no immediate danger from the Particle Accelerator towers. No fences or forcefields barricaded the public from the structures. There were no guards that protected the towers. People approached, but flux-fields were so intense that humans could not get within 50 feet of the Accelerators. The Media told citizens that the structures were indestructible and they were. Weapons had no effect on them and the energy was absorbed by the Accelerators.

It was explained to the public over Media how the black global grid of electrical towers functioned. The fantastic "Projector System" was unlike any Particle Accelerator that had ever existed previously. Before, these generating machines that tapped into the energy of a turning planet were *circular*. Particle Accelerators forced atoms that attained incredible velocities through TUBES. The Circle of tubes were massive in size and had to be to fool lightspeed particles, which made them CURVE. The new Phase II method operated very differently. There was no need for a perfect circle around the globe. Citizens were informed that the atomic particles *beamed* from one tower to the next tower on the Grid at lightspeed. [Ceana had a type of technology that beamed cargo and equipment over many miles]. Every time the towers shot particles to the next tower, they were sped up a little more. That increased the power more and more. When bits of matter were *pushed beyond lightspeed* was when the powerful/concentrated Super Energy could be directed to any point in the universe.

Ceanan society suffered and changed terribly because of the Accelerators. Darkmoor officials and State officials broadcast how lucky the blessed planet of Ceana had been during the entire millennium of Crisis. Ceanan citizens never experienced severe Holocaust problems of overpopulation that the rest of the galaxy had endured. *Maybe it was time for Ceana to suffer?* was in the minds of many.

***

Jain looked older and had short green hair now. She did not leave the planet as most others had. There were a few things the girl had to find out; she wasn't going anywhere. She used a flying-device strapped on her back and reached the peak of her favorite mountain. It was her own private place she named "Shera." She came here to sit, to think, to be alone or when she was very depressed. The girl did not want to flee in fear from a planet that she loved. She wanted answers. They were almost more important than her life. Like other brave-hearts, many citizens stayed and suffered the changes placed upon them.

She had a family trait and talked out loud. She said, "It's exactly like the Monster said it would be. Black towers with uniform vents and small green lights in twilight. This will feed and increase Planet Construction.

But in a later age, *everything will crumble to dust!* And nothing can stop it? Wow. No one realizes this, that it will happen? The magistrates must know it, ha, as Stripe said. But helpless to do anything about it?" Jain feared when she thought about the World of Tomorrow. She wondered: *Are we helpless against the inevitable and cannot do what's right anymore? Everything is a growing, out-of-control Monster and there is no hope in sight?*

Jain looked out at what was once a majestic landscape. Her special view. Now, her heart sickened. She nearly threw-up at the sight...

Ceana was once the sweet and colorful world of Jeff Blain's subconscious mind. But now, the real Jeff Blain was dead. It seemed his planet approached death. Ceana darkened and got colder. A perpetual gloom or haze that was only around the Grid of towers now swallowed all of Ceana. There was no bright day or black night. Now, there was only a grey vagueness or spooky sameness from the high atmosphere down to the ground. The Sun was only a dimly-lit circle that moved across a thick, cloudy canopy. The sky was not composed of clouds. There were no more slight changes of seasons. Weather patterns and Controlled Weather were very different now. AIN systems on Ceana still functioned, but drastically shifted to the mechanical and did not favor human beings. The trend was to cancel people in the long run. People were not important in the New Age. The overall MACHINE (and Darkmoor) was all that mattered. The *writing was on the wall*. In a matter of time, the one quarter of the population that remained, could not stay for too much longer. They had some time before conditions worsened. Presently, the situation was livable. But in the future, the Media called it: "electrical poisoning." More and more citizens left for Moon bases and other off-world colonies. Soon, Ceana inhabitants would be turned into survivors and refugees. Few people would be able to handle the coming harshness in the years ahead.

Jain cried when she remembered how beautiful and colorful the view was from Shera and now saw what was in front of her today: Six black towers that were hundreds of feet high, a few near and a few that poked above distant hills and valleys. The lovely grasslands and wonderful water systems of Trelaine and Ellebelle below her had lost their bright colors and were mere shades of grey. The water was undrinkable. Most colors of the scenic panorama were gone and a blandness took their place. The far hills of the Great Escarpment could still be seen, but barely. And her Moon! From birth, Jain always had a strong affinity for the lonely *natural* satellite. Maybe the reason she was passionate about the Moon was because she was a loner? She knew it was right there this time of "day," just beyond the blurry canopy, and it wasn't visible. The loner never allowed herself to fall in love or have a normal family. And now? It was all too late. Jain wiped her eyes.

"Don't cry," was said by a voice that she never heard before.

"Who, who's that?" Jain was startled. She first unstrapped herself from the flying-device, then rose to her feet and looked around. "Who's there?!" No one was there. She did a 360 and looked around one more time, and then she saw who spoke...

It was the clean face of a man who laid on a slab of rock and wore a full-length, white robe with a hood. "Don't cry," he repeated.

"Why didn't I see you the first time I looked around?" Jain asked and deflected his comment.

"I didn't want you to," the man replied. "That wouldn't be very surprising. *This* was more surprising, yes?" The man of mystery smiled. "Don't you like surprises, lady? I also have a bright, blue aura around me, but I didn't want you to see that either."

Jain smiled back and sensed there was nothing to fear. The visitor to her spot seemed *mostly harmless*. She took steps closer and sat on a rock across from the guy in white. She smiled and asked, "And who are you now?"

The man squinted, shook his head and also shook an index finger in the air in front of her. He wondered if she'd know his next words were a joke? "What, I have to give you all the answers, girl? What, you don't like a little mystery in your life?! What kind of detective are you?" He almost ranted. "I thought you enjoyed mysteries? Puzzles?! Why don't you freakin' tell me who you *think* I am, Jain, with no last name?"

She laughed. "Ha, ha, ha, you're a character, ha. Alright, ah...I don't have a fucking clue."

"There's a good, honest answer..." He winked at her.

She expressed, "I see. You know *my* name, but I can't know yours, *you crazy lunatic,* is that the way it is?!" She volleyed back to him like it was a good shot in a Roval match.

He replied: "You don't want to know my name. It changes. Well, we'll see if you can figure it out in the end, smart-girl, Detective?"

Jain suggested, "I should call you something..."

"Just not Late For Dinner. No. Call me, ah, AH...*the Man in the Mountain, eh?"*

"Are you not real? Am I hallucinating you? Did I take a drug and not know it? Did I create you in my mind...?"

The man's response was, "Other way around."

"What?" Jain was befuddled and tickled pink at the

same time.

He brought the girl down to Ceana when he sadly confessed: "I truly am very sorry about the ruination of your planet and the disintegration of Things to Come." Tears suddenly appeared in his eyes as if he was in far more pain than she was about her world. His right arm flicked forward for a second and he informed her, "I shouldn't have written it this way, but I did. That's what I'm sorry about. Very sorry about..."

Jain was struck by the man's odd words and quickly shifted into Serious mode. *Was he two people?* "Look, whoever or whatever you are, you must be here for a reason. So just tell me what you've come here to say. Spit it out..."

"No, it's Spill It. Alrighty then, I will. I know you still watch Media. The next big question pushed into the consciousness of the last remaining public is: Who built the Accelerator? You're a good sleuth, Detective. Who built it, really?"

"Who built it? I thought top State Scientists built it and it was all sanctioned by the State, by the HM? No? They didn't build it? Huh. You know, for a Wiseman of the Mountain, you should have more wrinkles and very long hair?"

"I have hair." He bent back the hood and there was considerable white hair. "It's a nice, modern cut. I like it."

"Okay, guy. Who built the damn Accelerator and why is it important? And, hey, how about: How can we change things so that what Dark Heart stated to the world won't happen?"

Man in the Mountain said, "You know the Devil says a lot of true things, that's how he hooks ya."

"Wait. I've thought about this for a long time now. It is more than obvious who built these fucking black things! The Horned Beast who first knew of it, told me and then told the world! That bastard was right. Everything has been turned to shit, since the start of the World Generator. Because this is exactly what the Dark Heart Center *would* do! Finish what he started a thousand years ago. Yes? Obviously!! Obviously, he built the Accelerator."

"Wrong." The man declared calmly.

"Wrong?"

"You'll figure it out, little girl, I swear to me. You'll know why it's important. In the end, you will know. Last Act? Aye?"

"Anything else, old man?"

"Ha. You don't know how true that is." He said, "We'll meet again, Jain. I guaRONtee. But for now, I have another program to get to. Thought for sure you'd know who I was. Oh, right, that was other Jains..."

"Other Jains?"

The man smiled, winked, blew her a kiss, snapped his fingers and disappeared>.

"Yeah, he's gone. Teleported away, did ya? *Program?* Did he mean: he had a program to see? Or. Am I one of his programs?"

***

Children of the Monitors lived and thrived on the surface of darkened Ceana more than they ever had before. These were suited, hatted creeps that often had no need for sunglasses now and displayed their big, black eyes. They relished the New Dark Ceana and the heightened Electricity in the air and in the ground. They had more and more energy and life. The original Monitors wasted away when global power levels were very low. They returned to the Darkness. These second generation and later generations of Monitors were different. They had no need for sleep. They were highly-charged by the Grid of Power whose tallest structures had grown to more than *300 miles in height!* The numbers of vampire-like creatures on the surface and in the underground would soon surpass the number of citizens left on the planet.

The atomic particle pathways or Vortexes between

the towers were intensified right along with the latest enlarged Towers. Citizens now observed perfectly straight lines of electro-magnetic flux between irregularly-spaced towers in the Grid. Red and purple were the prime colors of energy flows. It appeared that large lasers connected the towers in the semi-darkness. The small lights were green. The dramatic changes were results of the accumulation of energy that had increased minute by minute.

As far as the rest of Darkmoor was concerned, the World Generator that turned into a Particle Accelerator, *was a super success!* Power broadcast from Ceana truly quantum-leaped Planet-Building in the outer regions, every region in an ever-widening sphere. Construction of planets, moons and space stations increased by a factor of 100! Off-worlders were happy and the pressures of overpopulation had been relieved to a great degree. Very large populations had migrated to far more planets than ever before because of the increased Power Levels. These worlds were clean, fresh, "Paradise-Planets." They were all designed to be 'Edens,' miracles in space, fertile habitats, perfect environments that would harbor growth in the future for generations of refugees. They were the Promised Lands for pioneers and countless numbers of lifeforms. So far, the Accelerator Project and its Electricity-Beaming capabilities have been hailed by Darkmoor's citizens and elites. It was a "Positive" Particle Accelerator to those who had found fantastic homes and started new lives with their families.

That was not the case for the source of the Power. Nothing was "Positive" on Ceana. Ceana was a diseased planet. As off-worlds exploded with Life and the creation of one oasis after another, 'Jeff's Planet' corrupted - *changed.* Who knew how long Ceana would exist or could exist like this? An Ultra-Powered Planet, super-charged, more than anything had ever been before? The State's best psychic minds and machines projected visions of Ceana in the future and it was <u>a lifeless ball</u>. It mutated into a Mechanical World that served the galaxy as a Mega Utility Source, power beams that fed the needs of Darkmoor, not Ceana. Machines and the finest telepaths confirmed this view of Tomorrow and [strangely] never saw a destroyed Ceana, pulverized by overloads of Electric-Flux Forces.

TS Caladan

6 Man in the Mountain

Weeks had passed on Ceana (called 'Dark Ceana' by some) with situations that only worsened because of the maximized Super Tower Installations, of course. Global Media still existed, but its time was coming to an end. More citizens left the "blessed" planet that once meant: God is Merciful. Citizens changed the ancient motto to a more appropriate one for the New Age: *God was Merciful.*

Any human who remained on Ceana wore a small breathing-apparatus over their nose and mouth. They had to. Soon, more methods of protection from the harmful 'roentgens' and 'teslas' would be necessary. For now, the breathing devices were enough and they kept citizens (less than 5000 in total) alive. Dead zones had formed near the Towers. Presently, no life existed within 500 feet of any Accelerator. Not possible. In the first days of the black structures, life flocked to the Terminals as if they *gave Life* or greatly increased the elements and frequencies in which lifeforms flourished. Now, life-energy appeared *repelled* by Maximized High Levels of Power. Dead zones would only increase in the future with Terminals that heightened every day.

***

"Man in the Mountain? We're here (Shera) to see the Man in the Mountain? Is that right?" Dorsey giggled under her breathing-apparatus as she removed the flying-device from her back. Jain also landed and removed hers as well. They talked while inflight, but now they were on good old terra firma.

"Yep," Jain answered her girlfriend (the cool State scientist) through her breathing-device. "What, you don't believe me, Dor?"

"I'm always skeptical, you know that. If our world had progressed instead of this, they were soon to adapt beaming methods to people. Imagine us beaming to different places or teleporting objects like we've seen in movies, huh? So some guy appearing and disappearing isn't an extraordinary event, dear."

"No, it was what he said and the feelings I received when he said them. Why do I feel connected to him? Why the fuck am I still here on this dying piece of coal, this wasted/rotten planet!?" She got emotional.

"Easy, girl," Dorsey tried to calm her more than a good friend. "I'm still here doing research. Tell me why you're still here, Jain?"

"I think it's this dude! Like I'm fated, er, supposed to learn from him? He has the answers I have to know! I think..."

Dorsey stated, "You don't even know his name, who he is, what his game is. Maybe he's just an alien playing with you? Ha." She looked around. "So this is your secret place? If it was the old/beautiful world, it'd be a great make-out spot."

"It was." Jain went to kiss Dorsey and laughed because their breathing-devices were in the way. "Ha." "Ha, ha."

"Man in the Mountain is going to simply appear, is he?" she asked Jain. "Where exactly did he materialize?"

She showed her the slab of rock and suddenly...

He appeared just like he did the last time, no breathing-device. "Hi! Hey, if you two Fly-Girls want to snog, that's fine with me, Jain. Yer girlfriend's cute."

"Yeah, thanks." Dorsey seemed indifferent and acted as if she was uninterested in the clean-shaven man in a white robe. She asked him with a firm attitude: "How can you mess around, joke and carry-on when this planet is soon to be ripped apart?"

Jain had a serious face and looked to him for his reply.

He said solemnly, in a lower voice: "There is time. On that day, I will cry. I'm very close to Ceana...and you also." He stared at Jain and surprised her: "We're related. Thought you knew?"

"What? Wait...Who are you?"

"Yeah, I want to know too," Dorsey added.

"Naw, naw, again. You kids, today. You push a button and there are all the answers. They're not even the right answers. Work. You don't work for anything. Everything is handed to you. Some scientific detectives you are. (to Jain) How about exercising your brain, Jain, and you tell me who I am? Thought you were psychic?"

"I guess not when it comes to you, my friend," Jain said with a smile. "We're related, you say? Hey, old man, sure you can hear me? You might be going deaf in yer late years..."

"It's *you are*, not 'yer.' Did you get that from me, child?"

"Let me guess. See how close to the mark I am, Okay?"

Dorsey was intrigued.

Jain continued with: "Could it be that YOU ARE one of the original 20,000? You know, the original colonists on this, what once was utopia? One of my ancestors?"

The Man in the Mountain gave them a big smile as if she was correct.

Jain jumped to a whole new train of thought that she

had to explore: "Wait! When we first met you asked the question, as if it was a very vital question: Who built the Accelerator?"

The man stated, "You mean who built the Collider...?"

Jain said, "...Accelerator."

He corrected her with: "It's now a Collider." He flicked his arm almost like a twitch. "That's the way I've written it, anyhoo."

Dorsey smiled in a daze and shook her head, quite mystified. She only understood part of what the man said and will say. Jain too.

Jain was amazed at this whimsical *magic man* that seemed to have popped out of a very strange dimension~~. She asked a sensible question, "How's this going to end?"

He replied, "Ah, I think you mean something more than what will happen to this precious planet...?"

"I do?" Jain asked.

The Man in the Mountain responded: "Yeah, I think you meant a larger question: What will happen to you, to others, to Life in the Universe? Those are the right questions and important questions, yes?"

Jain replied, "Okay, great seer. Tell me specifically,

what will happen to me?"

He put his first finger on the side of his nose and winked. "Ha, ha. Well, to be honest...I have written that part yet..."

Dorsey and Jain turned their faces toward each other, made goofy expressions, then turned them back to the man.

Suddenly. The "dude" fiddled with an invisible device that was right in front of his face. His fingers hit buttons that were not there. He reacted as if something new and incredible had entered his own private, little world that the young ladies could not see. He was somewhere else and with them at the same time. The guy stated: "Wow! I've waited so long for Avatar 2 to come out in HD on my free movie site! Finally!! I'm sorry, girls, gotta go now! This is a little more important, Okay? I'll see ya again, for sure. You'll figure it out..." With a snap of his fingers, the man *disappeared!*

After a few silent seconds, Jain said: "Now I know what he is..."

"What?"

"Comic relief."

***

Off-Worlds had become much brighter and Ceana had become much darker. Yet, the Terminal Grid radiated - broadcast - transmitted more than 95% of the Energy utilized in the stellar systems of Darkmoor! And Increasing<. The Super Machine of Power was now the well-established "lifeblood" of the whole galaxy. Life in this small sector of this single universe completely depended on the Ceanan Accelerator. Why not tap into a Network that about all humans and aliens utilized? Why not feed off the Ultra Electricity? There was such abundance! Such POWER! *It was right there for the taking.* And systems had been extremely starved for energy over long periods of time.

How could the highest of galactic officials have not seen the inevitable? Now called a "Collider" in certain circles, how could any scientist or electrical technician be blind to the fated and certain outcome? In the past, the production of batteries was pushed. Each network, whatever they were, was independent. Also, when wired or wireless [broadcaster/receiver] Tesla systems were utilized, they too worked on a GRID principle. Grids were used so that if a problem occurred at any one point, another replacement piece could be plugged right in and the power continued uninterrupted...

BUT, if all of your Prime Power Systems ran off of one Power Pyramid, then, that (lifeblood) Broadcaster of Energy better be damn well protected because it served Zillions of Lifeforms! [This was how Atlantis, Egypt, Incas, Toltecs, Mayas, Aztecs Sumer, Babylon and even

Antennas (teepees) of the first Old West Indians failed and fell]. If all or most of your wireless (radio/TV) electrical systems were 100% dependent on one Power Pole or Power Station, *it better not be destroyed!* [WARS]. At that point of destruction, POWER WAS GONE, sky-vehicles did not fly, machines that everyone relied on, no longer functioned! No more anti-gravity! No more saucer travel "chariots" or lightspeed beaming! Power could not be newly-generated because ALL worked off the Prime Power Station for a long, long time. Other methods of electrical-generation had been forgotten, lost or made obsolete. Everything collapsed, back then...

The Ceanan Collider was a far, far worse situation than anything that had ever happened previously. Darkmoor systems had grown exponentially along with the Increased Energy Flow. Astronomical numbers of different civilizations only existed and thrived because of the Collider. [Surface black Terminals on the Power Planet had reached heights of more than 500 miles!]. If Ceana was torn apart by Electrical Forces and the System BLEW? **The devastation and death toll could actually far surpass what happened in the Great War!**

Scientists and psychics assured countless Citizens of Darkmoor that the Energy was contained and will continue to be contained in the future. Aliens and humans, for the most part, bought the idea that *Ceana's*

Forcefields will be enlarged and intensified proportionally as the Power increased.

Was Ceana blessed now?

The Machine was a Monster that *could not be turned off* and only generated more and more POWER every second! There were attempts to VENT the Super Accumulation of Electrical Energy. They were mere "bandages" to the growing crisis and only slowed the build-up to a small degree.

How could cosmic elites not have known? Actually, many State magistrates understood exactly what would happen. They knew perfectly well. And most of those guys left the galaxy or made preparations to leave the galaxy for safer havens in the Great Beyond. *Understand how a pressure-cooker worked, or, "If you put a bullet in a furnace, it'll explode."*

***

Once again, Jain traveled through the thick/electric air of gloomy Ceana with a flying-device strapped to her back. There was a difference: she had a larger mask on and goggles, as if a more powerful filtration system had to be employed. The obsessed girl was alone, a bit bored and wanted to see if she could attract and contact the Man in the Mountain again? Would he show up? *My long dead relative...*

"He didn't seem that dead to me," she said to herself

as she landed. She coughed. She lifted her goggles higher; she wanted to see how the scenery had changed with her naked eyes. "It's even a shade darker. Ha! I'll be. I see Monitors down there, a group of them, ha, and they can't see me. Cool..." Then Jain semi-screamed: *"Oh, my God!"*

A white bird had flown over her head and down to the canyon walls below~.

"That was weird, eh?" Jain expressed. "Can't be real. Right, right? That bird can't actually be alive. Someone is playing with me. What about my strange 10th generation cousin, an original colonist? Hell, how real is that? Oh, right, he's not, uh."

A part of the cliff crumbled in front of her eyes. Then, suddenly, the last thing Jain would have thought to have happened...happened. *There was a violent Ceanaquake!* It only lasted for three seconds. Other parts of the cliff face cracked and fell far below. She grabbed the wall, steadied herself and made sure the flying-device was not damaged. The girl had never experienced such a natural phenomenon. Only it wasn't a natural phenomenon. When the shaking stopped, Jain came out of her fears. She had heard of such things: They were called "Ceanaquakes." But they only existed in stories and in movies. Her 'spider senses' knew that this planetary instability was only at the beginning stages. It never happened in the real world and now it will occur more and more? She cried with those thoughts and with eyes that beheld her ruined Garden of a world.

"Don't cry," a softer voice spoke.

"Hey! Mountain man!" She turned to where the dude had appeared. She faced a surprise. It wasn't him, it was a her. "Ha, ah...who are you? I guess you won't tell me your name either?"

The tall woman had very long white hair and wore a white gown that shimmered in the light. She possessed a very brilliant, blue aura that covered every inch of her perfect body. She smiled a sweet smile and said, "My name is Aan. We have a mutual friend in common, Jain..."

"And who are you?"

"We've been called 'angels.' I know you don't know much about Archons..."

"I've met your leader, the Heart Center..."

The incredibly young (living) girl shocked the white (dead) goddess and the goddess semi-screamed: *"What? That can't be!"* Aan immediately closed her eyes, meditated and realized: "You sure did encounter our top Ranger, but the experience is only a dark spot I cannot see into..."

Jain replied with a big smile on her face, "And I

think we'll leave it at that, Okay?" She smirked like she 'held the cards.'

Aan was sure she'd be the one with the surprises. She was wrong.

"Heart erased the record of what happened, but not my memory of it. A place no one can see..." Jain pointed at the Archon's hair and said (out of envy), "I had hair like that once..."

"Really?"

"Yeah. At a costume party, I dressed like this nude lady in literature. I had a gown like that on. Huh, I looked just like you, uh. I guess he's not going to show, eh? Did he send you?"

"Ha, ha..."

Jain coughed and then questioned: "Why is everyone who appears here so damn happy?"

"I am sorry, young one. I thought of something funny. You are unaware that Jeff Blain's unconscious mind created the pretty, colorful world you knew when you were younger..."

"Who?" Jain asked. [She had no clue who JB was, his unique history or anything that had transpired in the distant past. Ceanan society had all been descended from the original colonists. She had believed her heritage was no different than anyone else's lineage. A lot had been lost after 10 generations].

"I laughed because of the thought: Jeff Blain, a first colonist, was miniaturized and was never enlarged. When his dream fabricated your real world of Ceana, you native inhabitants and everything else on the planet were also...*small-sized*. You are my size; you're not giants anymore. A relative oddity you should know, but it doesn't matter."

Jain changed the ridiculous subject and pointed at the panorama and got angry: *"That all mattered* to my people and look at it! I'm not supposed to be upset?! Or pissed? Been rippin' my hair out to try to understand. What are you, Mother Nature?" She wiped her tears. She slowly said, "Why can't anyone or anything stop this?"

Aan answered, "Maybe it has to play out, dear? What did he tell you was important: Your life, your end game, how you will wind up? The state of the galaxy, Life in general, everything that will happen in the Last Act, aye?"

Under her mask, she responded, "He said all that?"

Aan smiled. "He did. Ha. Please do not worry. Or try not to...Oh, here is something to ponder, Detective. See if you can figure it out, eh?"

Jain replied, "You sound like him, the designer of

my world."

Aan surprised Jain with her next words: "*I* am also related to you. What do you make of that, Jain?" White angel smiled.

"Hold on, sister..." The Detective used more of her 'spider senses' when she lifted her arms toward Aan and raised her hands. She received the fact that: "Yer not lying. But we are not blood-related..."

"That's correct," the Warmth confirmed. "It has to do with Jeff Blain's mother and the Moon. You are unaware that your Rose Moon is not a natural satellite. It is an ancient Spaceship, a famous one, at its central core. And I am, or was, very connected to that special Ship. So, in a sense, I have a strong connection to the Engineer's mother and the Moon. You do not have to understand..."

"Ah, I think you are wrong there, Aan. I very much do want to understand. I want to know everything!" The young woman in a breathing mask and goggles asked the goddess an important question: "Aan. Who Built the Collider? Who really created it?"

"Ha, ha." Aan laughed. She said words that she should not have said, "No fair jumping to the Last Act. And yes, that could be the prime question of them all for you, dear. A real Who-Done-It, eh? That one's on you, maybe the ultimate path to the Truth that you seek and that you have to figure out on your own? I should go..."

"Now *why* should you go? Why is it that, right now, you have to go?" Jain even wanted to know that little detail.

The Archon smiled. She decided to joke in the same manner that he did: "What, I have to tell you everything? What kind of detective are you, Detective? Some people work and struggle for answers. Ah, but I guess not you kids, today. You want everything handed to you...ha..."

"Ha, ha. Thank you, my Guardian Spirit. You made me laugh and I needed to laugh. I like you..."

"Me...you." Aan waved and faded into nothingness.

"Wait! Can you come back?!"

Aan did; she appeared just like she disappeared and looked at Jain.

"I'm a curious kind a gal. What was the Man in the Mountain doing that was so important that he couldn't show up? Do ya know?"

"He's watching a movie right now."

"I see. What's a free movie site?" Jain coughed.

Aan smiled, shook her head and was gone again.

***

One of the Monitors on Dark Ceana acted differently

than all the other vampire Children (later generations of creeps). It had the power of speech, but it made certain that it never spoke. It acted like any other creepy alien Monitor or pretended to. So far, THE DEVIL [Spirit of Dark Heart Center] who faithfully served Queen ZEP, got away with the grand deception.

The creature in fedora, black suit and tie (no glasses) boarded one of the last, sanctioned by the State, transport-vehicles off of Ceana. A forged "Multi-Pass" was flashed by the Monitor and that was all that it took to get it seated. Her Majesty sent it on another mission to a different galaxy. She hoped her spawn (eggs) would hatch and dominate another world as it had happened in Darkmoor. The big saucer would reach Andromeda in no time (4000 C-years). If the vile Monster was a true Monitor, under the skin, it would not have left in this manner and *traversed space and time*. No, the iso alien would have melted back into the Hell Darkness from whence it came>. This was no Monitor. This was the polar opposite of Heart Center, DHC. This was Hell and IT was hungry and wanted most desperately for its babies to consume another world...

The Beast blinked its big, black eyes. The bald Monster smiled and exposed its sharp, white teeth. IT missed the horns...

***

One more time, her special, high, mountainous,

make-out spot was revisited by Jain and her lover, Dorsey. They had no clue what would happen, *but maybe something extraordinary would happen?* was their thought process. The same mouthpiece and goggles had to be utilized, only this time much heavier (more protective) jumpsuits were worn. Their flights were somewhat slower because of the extra weight of the suits.

They landed and removed the flying-devices from their backs. The girls were not as mobile in thicker suits, but they were protected.

Dorsey asked, "Wonder who's going to show up this time?"

"Dunno. But this is almost fun. I can feel it, Dor. I'm going to be learning a lot from these spirits or whatever they are. Ghosts. Aliens. Really glad you saw one of them and know I'm not nuts..."

"Oh you're nuts, Jain. We both are to still be here and doing this."

Jain confessed, "I know why I'm here. It's what I do, the nature of my work. Why are you here, Dor?" She waited for an answer.

Jain did not see the smile, but her girlfriend smiled. Dorsey said, "I guess...I'm following you?"

The Detective expressed affectionately, "That's sweet."

"Don't cry," the Man in the Mountain declared and it was a joke. "I'm all choked up..."

"Funny." Jain joked back and asked, "You done watching the movie?"

"It was a tennis match..."

Jain asked, "What's a tennis match?"

He chuckled. "It's like Roval, only primitive. Never mind." He then said, "We should have more light." The man in white waved his hand and formed a pocket of light that cut through the thick darkness of electricity in the air. It was as if a spotlight was cast on the scene. "I'm like Mr. Natural..."

Dorsey encouraged Jain: "Tell him what you told me."

Jain said: "Alright. You're writing this? Nothing's real? This is a holographic program and yer the Programmer?"

"More like everything's real and I'm the Dreamer," was his response.

Dorsey asked, "How do you have the power to change reality?"

The Man in the Mountain answered, *"Because I'm freaking Jeff Blain, that's why!"* (to Jain) "Wait until you meet my mother. Oh, oh, oh, have you figured out who created the Collider?"

"You said *built it*," Jain stated as Dorsey watched wide-eyed in the spotlight. Jain had a great memory and remembered pictures, faces and words in her mind.

The spirit of Jeff said, "I've changed that chapter to *Created it...*"

"I see. Look...my distant ancestor..."

He replied, "We're closer than you think, kid. Maybe I'm your descendent?"

"Whatever. Okay, then. Great Film Director to this *movie* that surrounds us, darkly...why don't you just write us all a nice, happy ending, huh? Could you do that?"

Ghost of Jeff said, "What the hell do you think I'm working on?"

"Good," Dorsey threw in.

Jain asked with hope in her heart: "Then there's optimism, hope? The galaxy will succeed, not dissolve, decay and flicker out soon?"

Jeff's image told them: *"Oh, no. Yer all doomed. It's gonna Explode!* I'm still stickin' with that. Enjoy every second of life, kids. Before that time comes, it's gonna get even stranger around here and very soon. You haven't seen anything yet."

"Why are you doing this?!" Jain shouted at him in anger.

He was cool because of the knowledge he possessed. He knew or felt a few things that the girls did not. "Why? Why? Why? Big question. And a strange letter. Ah, because it's more *dramatic* this way? Yes? You must not be a writer. What are you, a freakin' reporter? One of my jokes. Hey, d'you know I'm not the same guy as before?"

"You are a confusing person," Jain said.

"I got another joke. Okay, Okay? Ask me, say these words: 'Gee, I hope the Dark Side never invades us again.' Go ahead. Say that to me..."

Dorsey said, "I'll do it. Gee, I hope the Dark Side never invades us again..."

The man delivered the punchline: "Narchon wood."

Jain replied, "I don't even get that."

"Oh, I got more," Jeff/Dan responded. "Here's one I stole, but you wouldn't know. Yeah, all this is a novel I'm writing. I write them in crayon...That's the joke."

"Funny. I didn't get that either."

"I'll say something for the Darkness..." The man talked more gibberish (sense).

"What?"

"We wouldn't be able to see how beautiful the stars are without it. Thanks, Jim."

Dorsey nodded.

Jain's comment was: "Almost interesting."

"I have to stop hangin' around with you puny humans. I'll never get into the Vulcan Science Academy! That's ah, more of my, ah...humor. I see it's lost on you."

"Tell us more jokes we won't get, eh?" Jain asked.

"I'll only give you guys one. Don't want to set you gals on an overload of hilarity. Although, yunze guys need a huge dose of it. Here it is: You know who the great Queen of Darkness is, right? Well, guess who her favorite Marx Brother was?"

"Huh?"

"Don't know? Then I'll tell ya. It was...Zeppo! *Zeppo!* [no reactions] Oh, jeez Louise, tough crowd. Not like when I opened at the Catskills. Here's one that killed: I normally perform for larger audiences. They're usually not midgets..."

Jain laughed a little.

"Ah ha!" he exclaimed. "I'm like Abed in Community."

Jain looked at Dorsey and admitted, "It was funny."

"I have a question..." Dorsey expressed.

The schizoid man totally ignored her and her question when he saw something that appeared on a big screen in his world that they did not see. "Oh, man!"

"What is it?" Jain asked. She and Dorsey were concerned. "What happened?"

He said, "The rain delay is over now and I have to get back to watching the match. Cool. Really cool, 'cos I was getting bored with you guys, you know? I mean..."

Jain was upset. "Really? Seriously? How rude. *What we had to do to get here!"*

"Ladies! It's the finals of the French Open! Try to be a little more patient and understanding, why don't ya? Huh? Gotta go! I'll see yunze guys soon. Oh, I'm also designing a ship. Space is so cool! Wait until you ride the Spaceways, baby! Bye."

"Bye." Jain waved and then looked at Dorsey's face. The Detective shook her head in disbelief. She expressed, "And this is the Joker I'm supposed to learn from? What the fuck, man?"

Dorsey asked, sincerely, "Are you closer to what you're looking for, Jain? Your answers? Why you are here? What you're seeking to know through this ghost-guy?"

Ceana

She took a few seconds and thought about the question. Then answered, "No. Not really. He said a lot of bull-jive and screwed up my senses, for sure. What the hell happens in Act Three? And, and he said that he was a different person than before...?"

"A Changeling?" Dorsey suggested.

"No, there's the same blood between us. And yet, I, uh, think I really like him."

7 The Cosmic Collider

If another word was connected to the "Collider," the word was "Cosmic," because Ceana's grid had evolved into a vast, all-encompassing, Universal Grid. The reference in Mega Media was now "Cosmic Collider" for the countless power networks that fed off of the Collider Source at the center of the system.

Darkmoor was less dark. The galaxy was much more populated than it once was ages ago. The number of different solar systems that utilized the Power Network was 19,140,074 and that number grew everyday! Individual networks of Electricity were uncountable since many more systems rapidly materialized and tapped into the Wireless Energy broadcast in space. The Collider became a power Beacon, a River of Energy that gave Life to an entire galaxy like a sun gave life to a planet.

"The next phase, Phase III, will be an even more incredible advancement for the Cosmic Collider!" *Third Stage will boost electrical energy to heights never imagined before!* Darkmoor's systems were changed and had evolved and had expanded to such an unbelievable extent that Officials over Mega Media considered that a "galactic name-change" might be in order? "The Radiant Galaxy," "Energia," "Centralla" and others were suggested. Even the idea that the new name should be "Ceana" was passed around the floor of the new Senate. So far, nothing has been permanently decided.

Even religions emerged around the enhanced, magnified, accelerated flow of Power. Few citizens of Darkmoor remembered the words of the Dark Heart Center or understood the great danger that was coming><.

There was a Problem. There was always a Problem. Long ago, reality on Earth was shattered. Then the Dream Reality was shattered. And then 1000 years later, Ceana was shattered. Ceana was the center, the crux, the place where the weird/boosted energy and energy-combinations focused on first. Later, the rest of the galaxy would follow. Presently on Dark Ceana, there were CRACKS in reality. Splits. Seams. Warps. Vortexes. Openings. Doors to other dimensions, alien worlds and other time periods, *swung open!* Not other moments in the prehistoric past of the planet; Ceana had no prehistory and came ready-made. But, there were real pre-histories, utopias, Paradises Lost, fantastic weapons and vehicles and old wars on other planets. Those true events that once occurred, as well as people and machines from other worlds, *poked through cracks and seams,* which now appeared on Dark Ceana. As time sped on, more and more lifeforms on Mega Media understood the true meaning of the (insider) word:

Ceana

'Collider.' In Phase III, the Amped-up Machine-Monster produced Worlds in Collision...

***

{Entitled: 'The Fruit Cellar'}

One of the first changes in reality was a harmless, sweet change in the life of Jeff Blain, the loner with the largest collection of PEZ dispensers. In this alteration of reality from long ago on an alternative Earth, Jeff never collected PEZ. PEZ dispensers, the candy and the collecting existed. But his fascination was placed elsewhere. He collected comic books. He loved comic books. He loved their wild, far-out stories. They "spoke" to him and he spoke back to them. Like someone who got lost in movies, the 5-year old easily lost himself in comic books. Comic books like DC's Superman, Batman, Green Lantern, the Flash and the Justice League.

Then MARVEL hit the racks in drugstores and ("Oh, my God!") little Jeff's universe had just doubled! *How is this possible?! I don't care, just keep 'em coming!* The boy was so thrilled, he peed his pants a little. His favorites from Marvel were Spiderman, Doctor Strange, the Fantastic Four, the X-Men and the Avengers.

He was obsessed with these ten superheroes and groups of superheroes. Only these ones. Not Green Arrow. Yeah, Iron Man was cool, but the boy wasn't excited about Tony Stark like his other favorites. Hulk was alright, especially when he fought the Thing. Jeff thought Hulk's comic book might not continue. *Yes! Can't wait for next month to come and where the 10 stories were going! They're fantastic!!*

There was a problem. There was always a problem. *Mother!*

Let's flashback to an "Origin Story." Jeffrey's origin story. How was it exactly that the boy got interested in comic books in the first place? Well. Jeff's father, Joe, drove them to grandma's house in Kansas to celebrate the boy's 5th birthday. Jeff usually "cleaned up." Not his room, but the only-child cleaned-up with many gifts on his birthday and Christmas. Right now, it was broad daylight. The car had little shocks and the trip had been a bumpy ride.

Jeffrey was in the backseat and decided to look at the comic book that dad gave him. It was the very young man's first comic book. *What's Justice League?* He wasn't that interested in it, before he examined it closely. His main thought was: *I got so many great things from dad and the aunts...and he tosses me this lousy comic book?*

The boy skimmed it for a minute and it still did not register in his mind because he was too busy wrapped in the thought: *What a crappy gift.*

"Hey, what'ju do, kid!?" The car swerved. The

vehicle almost went off the road.

Jeffrey, in the backseat, was startled and did not expect to be scolded by his father on their fun road trip to grandmas. "Wha ya mean, dad?"

Joe suddenly screamed: "I wanted that! You threw out the Justice League, issue Number One?! It's brand new. You know who's *in* the Justice League, son?! It was my gift..."

The boy shyly replied, "We, we can go back an, an get it?"

Joe looked at Jeffrey in the rearview mirror. "Not the point. I want to know this. Tell me right now, why'd you toss it, son?"

"S'was my gift. Not yours." He pouted. "*I looked at it.* I was done."

"Son, that was the first of its kind! Special. One day, it could be very valuable. There's a lot of new/cool ones jus' come out. A second, big, comic book company is in the works, and..."

"I never knew, you, you liked comic books that much, dad. Or, or at all?"

"I've always planned to show you my collection when it was time, kid. Then it would be your collection too. And keep in mind: a whole series of superheroes, from issue #1, right on through, wow! It's unbelievable what a whole series in perfect shape will be worth in the days to come, at conventions, festivals...yeah, for comic books..."

"Really, dad?" The boy was in awe, completely dazed during the rough ride. If father was so interested in them, *maybe I should check them out too?*

Joe looked at Jeffrey in the rearview mirror again. "Really, son. Love to see if they spark your imagination, like what they do for me, eh? They are only 10 cents now! If you want, that is if you like comic books, you know? It would be an investment, for your future. Believe me, we could be rich, I mean 30/40 years from now...but I need a little helper like you, son. I could drive us around to drugstores in our area, you can go in and buy the comic books you want..."

"Seriously?" The boy could not believe what he heard through his ears<.

"Yeah," his father said as his mind brainstormed even more. He thought of a plan that might solve a few domestic problems around the house. Mother complained that the boy never cleaned his room. (She was ill at the moment and at her sister's. Granny had to see little Jeffrey on his birthday so Rose was not with them). "I'll make a deal with you, son..."

"Dad? You dun even know if I'll like comic books."

Joe said, "I'm bettin' you will, ha."

"What's the deal, if I like 'em, of course?"

"Okay. YOU have to pay for them. That's the deal, Jeff."

"Dat's a lousy deal, dad."

"Ha, ha, ha, ha. No, here's what I mean. You have to learn to clean up your room. Look how many times mum has told you, huh? You do a little work around the house, clean your room, dry the dishes. Nothing big, rake grass clippings, that's all. And you'll earn an allowance..."

"How much?" (The boy wanted to know).

"Ha, ha. Let's see, now. How much we wanna spend each month on comic books?"

Little Jeff said, "WE? Ya said I'm payin' for 'em?"

Joe replied, "Yer gonna be a good businessman, son. No, I'll match you! Whatever you pay, I'll pay too. Even Stephen. How about five dollars for you working around the house? I put in $5. That means we drive around and buy the very next issue of your favorite superheroes and pay ten bucks, total."

The kid was a bit confused and expressed, "Dat's not very much..."

Joe *clapped* to get his son's attention. "Hey, SON!

Wake up! That's a grand total of 100 comic books each and every month! Now how we gonna slide our little plan passed mother? Mother, remember her?"

"Oh, shi..."

"Don't say that word..."

"I didn't say that word." Jeffrey was right. The boy was quick-on-his-toes and solved the problem, sort of. He informed his father, "We could hide 'em in boxes ina basement." [Pennsylvania and other eastern states on solid ground had basements].

The boy saw that his father's eyes looked away, while the man always had an eye on the road. He looked back. "Ha, that might work. Until she found 'em, huh?"

"There's lotsa room! It's cold, that'll keep 'em fresh like in the Norge, right? Right?" Jeff was excited! *He'd really have a business with dad!* Just the part of driving around to stores in the suburbs with dad sounded great. Like catching baseball.

Joe Blain laughed again. "You know, this could actually work, ha. You'd learn responsibilities; we can expand your duties as you grow up. We could use the help and I think mom would do *anything* that'd made you CLEAN. And it would all center on comic books. Hey, bud, how's it sound?"

"That's SWELL, dad! Yeah, it's a deal. I get my

choice? Right? Okay! And, and, sometime, I'd sure like to see your comic books...*our Collection, right?* How many do we have, dad?"

"Only 101. But they're good ones. It's a start."

With mother's permission, Father and Son went into the comic book business, the foolish, "stupid," comic book business. She put up with the boys' obsession. Rose was completely sure that they were "nuts," that they were "throwing their money away," it certainly was "not a credible investment" and "the basement is filling up with boxes!"

Joe and Jeff had the routine down: They knew the exact stops to make, a circuit that enlarged to more than a few drugstores: Bridgeville, Mt. Lebanon and Dormont. They didn't even have to go all the way to downtown Pittsburgh. Comic book prices had gone sky-high in 10 years and were now 25 cents a copy. It meant that the duo spent $25.00 every month, instead of $10.00 as it was in the beginning. Jeff's chores increased, naturally, and the boy did way more than the $12.50 that he earned. Father and son were very happy, together, in this activity/hobby that they both loved.

The boys couldn't buy the first issues of Superman or Batman. Those guys had been around for a while. Joe had some great ones in his collection, before Jeff. But the other DC superheroes were brand new; their comic books had just come out [updated versions of the old Justice Society] like Green Lantern and the Flash. They collected every Superman and Batman issue ever since Jeffrey was age 5. Each one was in sequence and kept in perfect shape sealed in plastic. It was the same for Green Lantern, the Flash and the Justice League. Only every issue from #1 and on and on in the series was preserved in plastic, then gently placed in boxes and stored in the Blain basement.

Then there came Marvel and OH MY FREAKING GOD! Could this "other company" with wilder superheroes never seen before, be *better* than DC Comics? Hard to imagine. *Be still my heart!* Marvel was the rage, a bold/new direction in comic book superheroes! The Blain boys were in their glory and only now developed their ultimate plan, the latest strategy, of precisely what they were going to do. The Plan:

There was one firm rule to the Blain's comic book business: 100 comic books were purchased each month, no more and no less. The boy chose 10 different comic book series, 5 from DC and 5 from Marvel. Only Superman and Batman would not be a complete series. (Few people had a complete set of Superman and Batman). Each month, they added one more issue, one more part to the continuation of 10 amazing stories and added one more number to a growing collection. Father and son loved their collection more and more as it grew<.

The books were really sealed well. Each one was sealed with great care and was absolutely 100% air-tight. Each large box was also sealed in plastic a few times and stored in the cold cellar. Each of the boxes contained 1200 comic books or exactly one year's worth of collecting. Do the math:

Ten comic book series of superheroes or groups of superheroes and each month the Blains returned with 100 comic books. They actually *bought 10 copies* of 10 different comic book series. It was not a single copy of 10 different series...it was 10 copies of 10 different series! And eight of them were complete, from issue Number 1. For every box stored in the cellar, the 10 series advanced by 12 issues. In 10 years, eight of the 10 series advanced all the way up to issue #120. And there were 10 copies.

The large boxes mounted up and occupied more and more space in the basement and in a fruit cellar that was attached. It was called a "Fruit Cellar," but it never contained much fruit outside of canned fruit on the shelves once. The many shelving units usually contained canned tomatoes from the big garden outside. That was years ago. The creepy, dreary, dusty, cold room also had old furniture and some of father's equipment that nobody used anymore.

Mother insisted that the old stuff be tossed out and the Fruit Cellar be used for the 12 large boxes. The cardboard boxes got in the way of her washer/dryer and dad's tools and work area that also occupied the basement. With the trash gone and the shelves gone, there was enough room for the dozen boxes filled to the brim with comic books. The Fruit Cellar was also filled to the brim and would now be known as the "Comic Book Room." For the boys' comic book business. *What business?* mother questioned. *They don't sell any! They just keep piling up! Oy!*

Nope, the boys hadn't sold one comic book or collection over the last 10 years of collecting. The art, the drawings, the stories, the adventures, were just too precious for the Blain boys. Their business was in the future. Money wasn't important to them. Love was important. They were thrilled being together in an activity that both of them enjoyed very much. Many fathers at the time (Vietnam) were not close with their teenage children. The Blains were different; they were very close.

They did give a few of the comic books away. Joe actually cheated and bought an extra copy of each different one every month. This was for him to read and also Jeffrey. The idea was to read the story, remember the story, and then give the book away. Jeff was a little more popular when he'd give them away to his few friends in school. He was known as the "nutty kid who gave his comic books away." He didn't mind; he had tons of them back home. His father felt the same way. It was their big secret. They had a secret business that might hatch in the future and no one knew about it but the Blains.

If this were real, the man and the boy would have made fantastic profits in 20 or 30 years with their comic book collections and mum would have had to "eat her words." They could have sold the complete series, #1 to #120, of Green Lantern, the Flash, Justice League, Spiderman, Doctor Strange, the X-Men, the Fantastic Four and the Avengers! As well as 120 early issues of Superman and Batman, in sequence, and in perfect shape! 10 TIMES OVER!! This did not happen because...

It was a dream

Jeff Blain *woke* from deep REM sleep~. He had been totally captivated and enraptured by the warm, warm memories of him and his father. *Memories that never, ever happened.* "Not in this world, ugh." Almost all of the dream was blotted out. It was very cold in the old house. He shivered. He slept with many layers of clothes on.

"This is not the first time I've had these kinds of ironic dreams that I do not appreciate, God! Thanks, again! Like that one vivid dream I'm mining for tourmaline and I find these beautifully colored, clear rods 4 feet long! I'm packing them away in this trench coat

I'm wearing and then I WAKE UP! Agh! Ah. Or the few times I've hit the lottery and then *I wake up?!* Damn you."

In the true world: The year was 2025 and Jeff Blain was 65 years old. Last night was the first night he'd slept in the family house in a half century. Mother had died 30 years ago. Father lived here as he'd done as a boy and as his father had done since he was a boy. This 794 house on Bower Hill Road was one of the first houses in Bridgeville. Jeff saw almost an ancient photograph of it once and everything was forest, no other houses were close to the area. He remembered a coal mine entrance across the street, but that was closed a long time ago. The man did not have many fond memories of his home and early childhood here. As soon as he could leave this small town where nothing ever happened, he was gone. That's exactly what happened. He wasn't close to either of his parents and was extremely pleased to "split for the coast" like many of his generation did. Southern California was the place! Jeff never looked back. He never had a homecoming and hardly stayed in touch with mother and father. His dad was a non-violent drunk. Jeff refused to come home when mother died. *Why?* "Because she never supported me in anything I've ever done in life." But, today...

The only-child had to handle the estate now that Joe had recently died. *HA, some estate! Little piece of land I can't sell 'cos it's the worst time in the world to sell with interest rates this high! No house is selling now and this dilapidated piece of shit is supposed to SELL!? I've been a failure all my life! Everything I've touched has turned to SHIT!! Had to take the worst jobs just to survive. Security jobs. Graveyard shift! Oooh, I'm the envy of my friends, huh? I never see snow and there's palm trees like I live on tropical Catalina or something?! Christ! How about you guys live with the cockroaches and terrible people around me, huh? I barely keep a roof over my head!*

Jeffrey said aloud: "At least I don't live here." Jeff didn't get much of a look at the place after his bus pulled into Pittsburgh's station last night. He took another bus ride, a local one. He was tired as he turned the key that he was given. He saw new bedsheets. He made the bed and went straight to sleep.

Now, in the day, he had a chance to look around at his "Kingdom of Dirt" that he inherited from his "loser" old man. The broken homestead had fallen into so much disarray and disrepair. What a Money Pit: it couldn't be sold and it couldn't really be renovated decently.

"What shit! Always had yer black cloud hanging over me, DAD! No fortunate son here. Thanks for all the great luck over the years, huh, bud?!" He kicked the banister at the bottom of the stairs and a piece broke off. "Ha. This is the story of my life! My writings, my art, my music, my games, my inventions, nothing has panned out for me! Got a lot to give and no wants anything from me!? Nice gift I have; *nobody wants them!* Why is that!? Now I'm retired and live on peanuts in a shit-hole. FUCK!!"

Jeff walked to other parts of the house. He was calmer and continued to talk or shout to himself: "I can't live here, in the cold?! I'm spoiled. Forced-air heating? It's terrible! I'll never be able to keep these big rooms warm in the winter. I guess I didn't mind when I was a lonely kid, but now? That bastard left me with NOTHING! Nothing in his safety deposit box. Checking and savings were cleaned out. What the fuck!? He left no insurance policies, DAMN. I have to now pay property taxes and inheritance taxes. I'm operating at a LOSS here! That's just typical. I always lose! *Jesus!*"

Jeffrey Blain hadn't seen what was down in the basement. He went down. He remembered the old stairs and they actually had a shower in the cold. Not now. "Some things have changed, I see."

It was freezing. He wasn't going to kick the furnace on and waste utilities. "I might be better off in a motel tonight and for the rest of the time until the funeral. God. God, *I've had such a fuck-up life!* Man. I actually thought...ah, I don't know what I was thinking..."

Then JB saw the Fruit Cellar door and noticed that it

had a lock on it. "A lock? Now why would it be locked? I remember that dirty/dusty room. Mum canned tomatoes. Well, I gotta see about this." Jeff saw no keys on the workbench or anywhere around it. He grabbed the old man's hammer and smashed the lock! The door opened...

"Ha, ha, ha, ha." He laughed as he received flashes of the dream he experienced last night. Jeff triggered more thoughts and kind of Moon-walked through the dream, backwards, and then remembered most of it. "HA! I was in business with Sir Joseph...the Comic Book business. Dad drove us to stores and it was our collection. Ha, ha, and valuable these days, very valuable, right, right?"

A big cardboard box stared him right in the face. It was that magic moment when you almost believed: *My lottery numbers will win.* "Sure, that's what the old man did secretly behind my back, eh? Yeah, he guaranteed my future by collecting old DC and Marvel comic books and stored them in the Fruit Cellar. HA! Sure he did."

Jeff did not venture into the room yet. He simply stared at the box that blocked most of the doorway and remembered the dream. *A coincidence, right?* Then he stepped up to it and thought to kick it. *Should I?* "If it's light and just an empty box, I'm still a poor boy. But, if it's heavy and filled with comic books, I could be one rich bastard." The first smile in a long time formed on his face.

Jeff kicked it! It was light and was just an empty, cardboard box. *Aw.* Jeffrey thought he was still a poor boy. He stepped into the Fruit Cellar, grabbed the box and was about to smash it into little pieces in pure anger. Then he saw...

A total of 12 large cardboard boxes wrapped in a few layers of plastic! Two rows of four on the left of the empty box and two rows of two on the right. He grabbed the closest one to him. "Gimme that!" It was heavy! *Was it comic books or junk?* He tore it apart and it was COMIC BOOKS sealed in plastic!!!

"I'll be a mother-fucker. Ha, ha. Superman, right on top! Superman #287." He flipped to the next one and it was Superman #288. Then there was Superman #289! He saw the Batman stack and it was the same: Batman #266, then Batman #267 and so on and so on. "Oh, I'm having a cow, man. Spiderman #1 and #2 and #3 and it was the same for eight more! And it goes to, and it goes to...?"

Jeffrey dashed to what appeared like the last box in the collection and tore it apart harder than he should have. His heart pounded and his hands shook. He discovered: "Yes, the series, all of them, go up to issue #120! From one to one hundred and twenty! *And that's multiplied by ten!* Get the hell out of Toon Town! *Dad,* you amazing man! You did this for me? You really did this when I turned my back on both you and mother? I'm so sorry for not being there for you two. I am very sorry,

Father."

The man collapsed on the hard, cold, stone floor. He hurt his knees. He didn't care. He could do many things that he'd always wanted to do now. He could make his dreams come true. It wasn't too late. He'd make changes. He cried and cried. The man had worried before: *Would I be able to show emotions during the funeral? Yeah, yeah, I'll be showing my...* Then he cried even harder.

***

In another reality, Jefferson Blaine opened the Fruit Cellar door and he soon discovered 12 huge, cardboard boxes that were filled to the brim with BASEBALL CARDS!! Ty Cobb, Babe Ruth, Willie Mays, Mickey Mantle, Roger Maris, Hank Aaron, Stan Musial, Roberto Clemente, Joe DiMaggio, Casey Stengel, Leo Durocher, Curt Flood, Vada Pinson, Ted Williams, Sandy Koufax, Warren Spahn, Nolan Ryan, Honus Wagner, Walter Johnson, Pee Wee Reese, Roger Clemens, Willie Stargell, Cy Young, Shoeless Joe Jackson, Jacky Robinson, Frank Thomas, Ricky Henderson, Lou Gehrig, Christy Mathewson, Satchel Paige, Frank Robinson, Harmon Killebrew, Ernie Banks, Reggie Jackson, Tom Seaver, Carl Yastrzemski, Whitey Ford, Mel Ott, Yogi Berra, Pete Rose, Barry Bonds, Sammy Sosa, Mark McGwire, Ken Griffey Jr. and many other cards of the greatest players of all time, in perfect condition. Times Ten!

***

On Pandora [real, inner satellite of what was once Saturn], the twelve-foot tall natives or "cat-monkeys" of the jungles were no longer blue in color. And the cat-monkeys of the seas were no longer turquoise. They had <u>unnaturally</u> transitioned to *shades of purple*. Ceanan and alien observers had not noticed the *great change*, but a few of them did. Prime concern on observing bases, presently: The entire planet with its fantastic eco-sphere that teamed with incredible varieties of indigenous lifeforms was tarnished and corrupted and diseased now. Why the sudden and harmful climate changes on Pandora? The answer was obvious to scientists and other observers. The Saturnian satellite was much too close to the electric rays of the Ceanan Broadcaster!

All stations and bases and places where there were living creatures within a radius of 500,000 miles around Ceana, were affected by the electrical flux of energy similar to atomic radiation poisoning. It was a semi-dead Sphere. Nearby planets, moons and stations were abandoned.

In the outer reaches of Darkmoor, there was the appearance of perfect - power - precision and distant Life thrived and utilized technical wonders never experienced before! More quickly-fabricated (natural) Paradise-Planets were produced and more tribes of humans and aliens inhabited them. Outside of very small/negative incidents during clashes of contact between alien colonists, there was PEACE. Colonists had more electrical energy than they could ever have used. They had high technology and great power was at their command. There was room, plenty of wonderful/clean nature to be expanded. Wide open spaces of beauty and abundant resources for colonists and their families to live and live well! Tomorrow appeared very bright. ...*But only if you were lightyears away from the Prime Power Station.*

***

On Dark Ceana, any living organisms no longer heard a hum in the atmosphere, it became a quiet roar<. When any creature was near the surface or within hundreds of miles of space, they had to be adequately protected in what was called "Still-Suits." They resembled deep-sea diver's suits, with helmet, and were composed of very thick materials. Still-Suits were especially designed to shield against massive amounts of electrical and magnetic energy. Users breathed from filtered systems, ate protein pills, drank from a continuous/slow water supply and automatically ejected bio-wastes.

The landscape certainly had transformed to a darker sphere and one much more deadly. Conditions resembled night, but it was not night. When the few brave souls who remained in this super harsh land saw the Power Grid

Terminals on the surface...

They primarily observed the very bright red and purple (laser) lines of the EM Vortexes between the Towers. With such negative-energy darkness over all of Ceanan's topography, observers hardly distinguished the titanic Terminals that reached more than 500 miles in height! But. Darkness was not everywhere on the Power Planet:

The CRACKS, the seams that now appeared larger and larger between worlds, were not dark. They were light. They were very bright lines. Certain locations on the Power Planet now had ridged, angled, geometric lines that widened. Triangles of light spaces moved and were very brilliant in some cases. The geometric spaces were *negative spaces* or OPENINGS. In time, the spaces widened and enlarged to greater degrees. The bright Openings became part of Ceana's landscape. There weren't many lifeforms left that noticed the angled portals/doorways.

Cracks in Reality were viewed by hordes of Monitors that roamed the lands like vicious, wild animals. The creatures had grown in size somewhat and definitely in strength. They ran in packs and often on all-4s. They were far more dangerous now than ever before. But who was there for them to terrorize and eat? Three human beings remained on Ceana and *that was it.* The Monitors were not Monitors anymore. Before, they were weak creatures of the shadows, minions who waited to be commanded by higher Evil. Today, they were smarter. Amped-up. They didn't wear fedoras, but still had jackets and ties. They were independent and strong, electric, Monsters of Darkness that were anxious to consume new worlds and kill any lives that were not like them.

What new worlds were these through the elongated and brightly-lit triangles that appeared in the Darkness of Ceana?

A group of brave (former) Monitors that numbered nine approached one of the very large, triangular Openings. Their leader put on its black glasses and motioned for the other eight to do the same. They did. Slowly, they all approached and got closer to the portal/doorway that was not there. Even closer. The leader was right at the edge of the bright Window.

The old "Children of the Dark" would never have had the courage, or even the thought, to act and motivate themselves into the Unknown...but this Next Gen Monitor would~. The bold leader with the jacket ripped by its new chest muscles, straightened its tie and entered the Window. It was more of a crawl-in than a step-in.

...Once the creature was inside, it saw that everything around it was a bright, alien universe! The big triangle (the way back) was very black and a tiny part of this new universe with...

Grassy hills, a wide river, distant snow-covered mountains, blue skies, a few billowy clouds and what appeared like a crystal-clear lake in the foreground. But the creature in dark sunglasses had its hand next to its eyes as it tried to realize: *What were the strange anomalies scattered over the new landscape?* Machines. War-Machines in ruin? They appeared very damaged, pock-marked with holes, rusted, as if from another time. Yet, the weather was fabulous, the water and skies were clean and clear.

The Monitor creature actually had the sense that the odd, grey, mechanical things in view were from very long ago that the vegetation had grown around it and purified itself. But as to *why* these bright spots or universes now existed on Dark Ceana, it had no idea. The quasi-vampires did not possess the intelligence yet to understand the cause. And the cause of Everything bad had always been **The Collider**.

The leader felt a breeze on its light-grey skin. It had more confidence when it observed and sensed that there was no life in the area. It raised its arm and waved to the others for them to come out (or in) too. A few of the bald bastards pushed just their heads over the line and through the portal. They growled. They checked their database. They felt better, more courageous, more comfortable, and also crawled into a new world...

Only three of the creeps. Five were not that brave; they stayed on the other side and *guarded* the entrance or the exit, whatever. The leader possessed 2 stripes on its jacket and its trio of crew members had 3 stripes on their jackets. Two stripes remained silent, but stuck its arm out and indicated: *What do you think of the place, boys?*

One transmitted a telepathic and digital response: *Way too bright. Way too pretty. Not the old machines. Strange machines. Not in database.* The two other minions nodded in agreement.

Let's explore? the leader relayed.

Good.

The four creeps in ripped suit jackets trekked (not crawled) over lush grasslands in the direction of the lake and to where the closest mechanical tower was located. It stood 90-feet tall right on the shoreline with rotten valves and tubes. The bottom part of the tower was rusted. Sections of the silent apparatus were not there or were removed. Pieces of it laid on the ground around it. Very high up on its side was painted: "**023**." The number was near a glass aperture or lens that was within a slight indentation, circular in shape. They saw that the next closest tower's lens, which was near "024," was cracked and broken. The lens on the tower in front of them appeared intact.

What purpose would those mechanical towers serve? *the leader asked the other three minions.* It was an intelligence test.

A minion quickly suggested: *Surveillance. A network of spy towers to view the approach of enemies?*

Another offered: *The network could have maintained a forcefield wall where no enemy could pass?*

Leader Monitor asked the last one for its digital thoughts. The group were only 50 feet away from the tower and shoreline.

Its reply was: *More than surveillance or forcefield, it could also contain defensive capabilities, such as...*

A YELLOW RAY shot out of the intact lens of tower #023 and it *vaporized the minion that spoke!!* It shot out three more EM Pulses that also de-materialized the other three Monitors! Normally, they would have absorbed the energy like how the black Terminals in the Grid could not be destroyed by powerful weapons. But on this side of the "mirror" and inside another world, the realm-space through the Cracks, the Monitor Monsters could be destroyed.

***

A 2-stripe Monitor that had grown in intelligence, stole a high-tech spyglass from a corpse that it found and ate. At the moment, the glass was used to peer through a wide, triangular Crack in the blackness of Dark Ceana. The creature kept its sunglasses on. It spied into another dimension that thoroughly amazed the semi-smart creep. It opened its mouth in awe. The brilliant universe confounded the electric vampire of the Night. The Monitor stayed put and just *drank* in the Undiscovered Country in front of it. The Watcher watched and it observed:

Children. Two blonde, human children no more than twelve years old. They were in a field in what seemed like the middle of the day. They played with a piece of 'modern' equipment that appeared too large for the children. The machine was a mechanical Gundam, dark green in color and designed for adult-sized users. There was much wear and tear on the "walker" as if the mobile legs and chassis were very old and hasn't budged in a century. The kids appeared happy and excited, like the unit was a new discovery to them. They climbed on the ancient mechanism that seemed so out of place among the trees and small settlement [fortified bunkers] in the distance. Further along the pink horizon of the planet or moon, stood a spectacular mountain range.

Suddenly, the Monitor noticed a change in what it viewed through the spyglass: The boys turned and saw a hovercraft that dashed their way. The vehicle arrived on the scene, next to the Gundam, within seconds. Out emerged a blonde male and female in very modern clothes while the driver stayed inside the vehicle. The Monitor believed he witnessed *parents who disciplined their children for playing on a thing that was dangerous.* The man swatted both young ones in the rear, lightly, and they got in the back of the hovercraft. The "parents" acted frantic, very worried. They looked in a few directions as if a threat was in the area. Soon, the adults were in the flying car too. The vehicle drove back in the direction it came, where the bunkers were located.

The *show or drama* for the Monitor was over. It only observed fields of wheat that blew in the wind. Minutes later, a flock of seagulls flew over a forest on one side of the view. Not much else.

It asked itself: *Why would they act fearful?* Then told itself: *I'm tempted to walk in.* It was more than tempted...it walked in. Brave boy. Curious. All was bright in every direction and the extended, black triangle was the way back. *I see.* First, it crawled, then found there was no problem when it walked upright. It walked and walked. Closer and closer to the bunkers. *Why were they so fortified?* The pale, bald creature had to find out...

Then it saw it. Far, far, in the distance, on the highest mountain peak was a *gigantic Lizard!* Its length had to be more than two miles from snout to tail, bright green in color. The Night Creature never saw anything like it before and searched its database. *What to do?* It could have made a mad sprint back to the portal? It decided not to do that because of how far away the monster was. It did not see or sense the little creep, so the little creep felt comfortable. It felt at ease and was in no danger. Instead of a fearful run, it leisurely strolled through bright wheat fields. It felt a strange feeling: It felt...nice. It felt good. Not paranoid. It smiled. *Could this weird place change me? Would I not want to savage and consume the first blood-filled human I encountered?* It didn't think that it would and marched forward. At least, it understood the actions it observed. The family was worried, probably because there were giant lizards that prowled these lands and the children were out past curfew? For a short time, the creature felt happy. It was an overwhelming sensation and he wanted, he wanted, he actually wanted to meet a person or creature in this new world and just say: "Hello." To have any type of meaningful, real experience with Something. It did not matter if they communicated. Simply to feel what They felt? To be touched, to know what that was like. Only for a moment. It would be cherished by Mister Two-Stripes. Maybe I could change? *Maybe it could happen in this sweet, bright, colorful universe?*

It reached the bunker and it heard a noise. ~*Slam*~ A portal door unlocked and opened. It was people! Seven humans came out just to see the visitor. Two old folks, two middle-aged humans and three children. They had happy faces! They smiled! The people wore old-fashioned clothes from the 19th Century* [*database reference].

The Monitor didn't think there would be any common language with the natives and there wasn't, or didn't appear to be. They seemed mute, so the Monitor stayed mute as well. Everyone was happy as if they welcomed one of their relatives back into the fold. The creature felt *feelings*. It was wonderful! They grabbed him; he felt their touch and it felt fantastic! Then it heard MUSIC! The family wanted the bald guy to dance and the weird creature *danced!* They all danced and clapped their hands. The Monitor really relaxed as if it was drunk* (*) and loosened his tie. Hell, he took it all the way off and threw it as far as he could! This was the greatest experience in its dark, dark life! More potent than any drug! Or better than the killing of prey. Without a word spoken, they made the creep a member of their family. It appeared that way on the surface.

The oldest male waved his hands and the music and dancing suddenly stopped...

But not the creature. The Monitor danced its bizarre dance a little while longer. It was hooked and wanted the gaiety and the joy to continue. When it came down from the clouds, it looked around and saw that the people were still, motionless, and no longer had happy expressions on their faces.

The faces were mean, terrible faces. The Creature of

the Dark was frightened. Then suddenly, over a green hill, *a giant Lizard appeared and roared!* Now the Monitor understood the odd actions of the family from the fortified bunker and why the music and happiness stopped. The two-mile long monster roared again and stepped towards them and created the loudest of sounds!

The Monitor was certain the family would run in fear back inside the bunker. No, it was surprised and observed the oldest male with a big, black book in his two hands. The man from the 19th Century conjured a witch's spell from a Spell Book. He raised a withered, old arm high over his head and screamed the words: "Moloch Deus!"

The power of the spell was like a lightning bolt directed at the great Lizard. The Monster was changed into yellow smoke and only *crackling* sounds were heard. The imminent danger was over.

They were saved! Saved by Magic. Or were they? The Monitor returned to the happiness that it had felt earlier. It stretched out its arms, rubbed its bald head and tossed its jacket and glasses away with a twirl. It felt waves of warmth from behind, where its new family stood. It felt fantastic! It felt loved. Like its family won a major battle. Now, *celebrations!* Monitor sensed the family would celebrate with a big feast...

When it turned around, all seven of them opened

their large mouths and showed very long teeth and fangs. The Monitor was not a dinner guest. It was dinner.

**

A dumb Monitor walked a long walk, a very long walk, to one of the black Terminals on the surface of the Prime Power Station. The Towers had reached unbelievable heights of over 800 miles above the surface! The stupid Monitor trekked the distance of a hemisphere, halfway around Ceana, just to TOUCH a Terminal>. If it touched it physically, the creature would gain more energy (like an amphetamine rush) for a short time, truly. The new 4-stripe creep finally made it to what was the closest Terminal-Tower. Its Great Odyssey was over! It would *drink deep* the Power and the Energy and the Glory in utter Darkness.

The scene was not totally dark because the lowest red and purple Vortex, laser-line of Electro-Magnetic Energy from the Tower, was only a few steps away and illuminated the area nicely.

The creature was ready. Its big, black eyes blinked. It never sweat before, but it sweat now. It wiped its face. This was it. This was the moment. It would do it...

It leaped and got a good, hard grip on the Power Pole and never let go! "Aaauiieeeee!" The RUSH was divine, majestic, supremely pleasurable, sensations never realized before! It shook. It violently vibrated with every roentgen or tesla-wave that pulsed through its enhanced 4th Gen body! "Aauuuwaaaaayy!" Then the creature let go and fell to the ground. It was all too much. Its legs buckled. It never dreamed the feelings, the high, would be anything like this! Ecstasy! It had to *do it again!* It was fine. It lined up another leap to the Power Pole and got a little dizzy from the endorphin mega-boost. It staggered backwards, tripped on rocks, and as it fell backwards...

The Monitor's head came in contact with the lowest rung, the red and purple Vortex-line of EM Super Energy and *the force immediately obliterated its head!* Its body jerked and then fell dead, lit by the thing that killed it. That was one way to destroy a Monitor in the Dark. The 4-stripe creature was not very intelligent. Its Monitor buddies told him how fantastic the high was from the Terminals, but they failed to tell him: DON'T TOUCH THE POWER LINES!

***

Not even the highest of galactic Officials and their Ultra Machines or the greatest psychics minds understood the true horror of the Monitors...if they were not stopped or somehow contained. Since they were ISOS, they were not a part of the normal elements of our reality. They were composed entirely of another type of substance, a much darker one that acted funky. No matter what might occur with the destruction of Darkmoor via the inevitable OVERLOAD of the Ceana Power Station...

The Monitors were stronger and stronger by the minute because of the Amped Collider. It was a crisis in the making that no one saw coming: **The Super Monitors!** The spread of the Newly-Charged Legions of MONITORS must be dealt with or many more galaxies will succumb and fall to the dark Contagion. Robot Armies were posted far from Ceana, yet still made sure no Monitors ever left the Prime Power Planet.

The Power Station, with its Mega Electricity and Magnetism, produced another galactic "cancer," called Monitors. In the long run, the Monitor Contagion could be far worse than the Contagion of 'Giant Nanites' or the menace of 'Replicators' or Tribbles.

***

A 70-foot orbital craft, retrofitted with "High-Impact" EM shielding, slithered through the heavy fields of Ceana's low atmosphere. The weird sky-vehicle looked like a turd in the darkness. It had bright lights that lit the way. The rounded bulkheads were built to endure the pressures of the Sun's corona. The passengers were safe. The orbital craft was manned by two girls, Jain and Dorsey. Each was dressed in Still-Suits. They slowly, ever so slowly, headed for Jain's special spot in the high mountains. That is, if they could find its coordinates on the ship's computer screen among high EM levels and all of the static? They believed that was where Jeff Blain would appear again...

Suddenly. Inside the shielded ship that skulked through thick air, the girls heard:

"I should just get this over with. It's not even my chapter anymore, huh?"

The gals, in what looked like deep-sea diving gear, were startled at words that did not come from the communications system. They shouldn't have heard the words, but they did.

"...Or maybe I should have started by saying: 'Don't cry'? Say, where are you ladies from? OH, poop, I'll take them away." The Man in the Mountain flicked his hand and their heavy, cumbersome helmets disappeared.

Jain and Dorsey freaked and gasped for breath! They knew the air in and out of the craft was electrically toxic and they had to breathe through the filtration system. *They freaked out more.* Their eyes enlarged and were filled with *terror!* They bent over and tried desperately to breathe...

Jeff said, "I don't get girls. Or maybe it's just you two I don't quite understand." Then he yelled at them: *"What are you two doing?!"*

Jain and Dorsey (not so) soon realized it was all in their minds. The air was fine. Jeff changed it. In a few seconds, the ladies breathed normally.

Jeff thought it would be more comfortable without the 50 pounds of Still-Suits they wore. He twitched his hand and the heavy suits were *gone.*

The girls were completely naked. Awkward~.

Jeff reacted. "Ah, too cozy. *Oops.* Uh, sorry 'bout that." He flicked again and said, "There you go. Uh. That was nice." Skin-tight, grey jumpsuits covered their fine, young forms. "Okay, now. I'll ask again. Where're you girls from?"

"Huh?" They were about speechless, totally bewildered at the guy and the strange reality around them that he, apparently, controlled.

"I mean, I mean, you don't live on this Turd Ship, you called it, right? I mean, where ya sleep? Where do you eat and hang yer toothbrushes, you know?"

Jain asked him, "You want an answer?"

"Yeah, gimme a real answer," (a different) Jeff Blain asked. "I haven't figured that part out exactly."

Dorsey spoke for Jain. "We bunk together at a small orbiting base that's EM protected with my associate. We three are the only ones left." The girls sat on the ion-insulated seats and tried to grasp what was happening.

JB didn't believe her and asked, "Are you sure about that?" He smiled big.

"Yes." "Yes."

"But how d'you gals get from your base to the Turd Ship, which isn't a spaceship, and back again? That's like a little plot-hole I haven't figured out, eh? Oh, I'd be fascinated with the answer to that question."

Jain told him to: "Turn around."

'Blain' did and saw a mini-Stargate. "Oh, how cute! Very convenient. Too convenient. I don't think I would have thought of that, huh? Really cute. Now wait, I'm puzzled and have to figure out every mystery. That's *alien* technology that you guys don't have yet..."

Dorsey replied, "Our associate brought it in. He's Andorian. The little stargate beamed through a big Star Gate."

Jeff laughed at the oddity and the fact that Things Tended To Work Out, like they're not real? Like, out of his control? That's not right and he wanted to get to the bottom of it. He felt a rant was about to burst from inside him: "This blows my mind girls, because I thought I was writing the story! I thought *I* was in total control, aye? After all, it's only *my* Afterlife. It's not your Afterlife. I'm the one with the remote control device, I mean. I'm the Dreamer. They've even called me the Creator, so WTF! There should not be one single item in this, in this, in this, crap, I've forgotten that word right now. That's another thing; I shouldn't be forgetting ANYTHING!

Almost said 'Nothing.' I never thought of the mini-stargate through a big Star Gate, but you did Jainy. Now, think about this. You think about this now. Since when do you have the power to program my Program? Don't answer 'cos I know lots more than you..."

"Uh ha."

"I'm writing the story! You can't be writing the story...unless..."

"Unless?"

JB eased on the throttle of his endorphin rush, or was it adrenaline? He answered, "...Unless we really are related like twin, twin, twin, ah, I forget. *Ah!* I don't just mean being from the same planet, I mean in the biblical sense, aye?"

Jain was speechless.

Dorsey expressed, "What? And why are you acting all goofy? You are really acting whacked, man. Why is that?"

"Okay, Miss Scientist. It's because I'm of two minds right now. Sometimes I'm Jeff Blain and sometimes I'm his next stage or new person coming in..."

"Who's that?" Dorsey asked.

"Someone not Jeff Blain."

Then Jain was not speechless. She expressed: "Ha, ha. DUDE! Just tell us what's going on, Magic Man!"

"You really wanna know, Detective?"

"Ugh." "Ummmmmm." Both gals sighed, looked down and then looked at each other and smiled.

"You believe this guy, Dor? Hey, you sure you have time to tell us? There might be a Soccerball game on or a Flog match or the finals of Roval or Ring-Rong!"

He frowned and replied, "We don't have those kinds of cool futuristic games, girls! We're stuck with boring baseball, racing and golf or girl's high school basketball or rugby and cricket on weekends! (looked away) NO, Don't put a *Lakers game* on TV anymore or the Steelers! You bastards! Hey! I'm not payin' for yer Sports package!"

"Who are you talking to?" Jain asked.

"You'd be surprised, sister. But I like to save my surprises for the end..."

"I don't understand the words coming out of your mouth," Jain admitted.

"That's from a movie. That's where you got it from and *you don't even know!* And I already used that line in the first one. You know...you two...you have to better control yourselves more. C'mon, help me out, eh?

There's only a few pages left..."

"In what?"

"In the story," he replied and rolled his eyes.

"Okay." "I see." (They didn't)

"...So, so, why am I asking 'cos I know the answer? D'you figure out who created the Collider? You know, the thing that's caused all the problems 'round here?"

Jain shot out the first answer from the top of her head: "YOU did!"

Jeff quickly and emotionally responded, *"Lucky guess! No way! Who told you that?!"*

"Gotch ya." Jain winked and didn't know why.

"We'll see who got who, *Superwoman.*" He pulled out a black, tubular device like a thick pen and held it vertically in front of the girls. He pressed the top nozzle and out ejected a small mist. Jeff realized it was the wrong tube. He sniffed and said, "Ah, the patchouli." He told them, "Just be glad it wasn't the Red Rum, eh? Ha, ha."

Dorsey and Jain shook their heads and laughed, but they didn't get the joke. Both expressed in different ways: "What the hell are you doing, man?"

"Okay. I'm gonna spray you two a little with that

thing from 'Men In Black.' Pretend you know what I'm talking about. *They do.* Now, it'll make you forget for a short time..."

Dorsey was leery and cautiously asked: "That thing will make us forget?"

"Yeah, yeah, I can do that anytime. It's safe. *Mind-wipes are safe!* But here's my joke, here's my joke, Okay? I got a joke for ya! Alright? Now I'm one of the agents in suits and you've witnessed a crazy thing yer not supposed to see, right? I pull out the Forget-Me-Stick and spray it at ya, ha, but the nozzle is turned towards me, see? So when I spray it, it hits me right in the face and I say... "What the hell was I doing?"

"Ha, ha."

"...Kinda like what you just asked, *what the hell am I doing?* Eh? (to Jain) You laughed," Jeff said.

Jain stated plainly and succinctly, "I was laughing at you, old man."

"Hey, since when are there 3 'c's in 'succinctly'? I know there were always 3 'n's in 'annointed,' but now there's only 2? Hmm. Must be another one of those pesky PEZ-Effects, aay, girls? And who wants to deal with those little items, right? I mean, who wants to be reminded that the world makes no sense anymore, yes? Ha, ha, *PEZ-Effect*...I'm so glad I thought of that, or I never would have written...*hey, I know!* Before I answer your questions, how about I use the Spray on you? Glad you guys agree. Before I hit the button though, ha, I gotta tell ya. Boy, are you guys gonna laugh. You didn't have to hire the Turd-Mobile and travel through HELL to get to me. Even the flying backpacks you used; all that was completely unnecessary. It was a waste of time and effort. I swear, gals, I was gonna write it where I come to you on the orbiting base. I swear it's true. I'm not in control. You shouldn't have jumped the gun, guys."

"What?!"

Jeff pulled out the proper black stick from his white outfit and aimed it at them and *hit the nozzle.* The light flashed and the girls totally forgot what had occurred over the last couple of minutes.

"...Sort of like what happened in that old Hercules movie, but you don't know that yet. I got LOTS of things to show yunze! Have any questions? Oh, I have one! Who conceived of the Ceanan Collider first? It's like the same question. Hmmmmm?"

Both dazed and mind-wiped ladies didn't know and did not offer an answer.

"That's better."

Jain spoke: "Ay! I just realized something, Jeff Blain, my long lost ancestor! You're DEAD!" (Why did it only strike her now?).

"I know I am, but what are you? Ha, ha. Okay, see...I'm hidin' the blue aura." For two seconds, he flashed the light and then took it away. "Why show it? We're not different. I'm no angel."

Dorsey only now grasped the fact that this was not an alien with powers who messed with them. It was a real ghost. A dead guy. She inquired, "Have you written the ending to our lives yet, Mister Blain?"

He told her the truth: "Well, I'm not him anymore. To answer, the *very* end of the story is done, but not the last chapter that leads to the end. It's not finished yet."

"Say, Mister Man in the Mountain, ah, what's going to happen to me in your epic? You know, my character?" Dorsey asked, nervously.

The man replied, "I'm not sure, exactly." He rubbed his chin and said: "I was going to write you out. But on the other hand, since you are a cutie, I think I'll keep you around for a while, eh?" (winked).

Dorsey laughed, "Ha, ha."

Jain asked the dead guy, "What's the last chapter called?"

TS Caladan

8 Who Created the Collider?

|It was a dark and stormy night. *No.* Once upon a time... *No. Start again~~~*|.

What existed deep within Ceana? The spherical DYNAMO Station, the Prime Power Planet that was the center of All Electrical and Magnetic and Magical Things...

What was at the planet's exact center? The core? The original, rich soil of Ceana hardened during its metamorphosis over time. With every roentgen-wave and tesla-frequency broadcast into outer space, rocks/dirt/soil stopped being rocks/dirt/soil. Minerals fused together in the intense underground, the Electric Heat, and became an amalgamate of natural elements. Ceana's crust and mantle became denser and denser and heavier and heavier as time clicked by. "The best electrical conductor was a hollow metal sphere," so the planet mutated into a Heavy Metal Ball with a hollow core. Dark Ceana had an empty sphere in its exact center.

After a certain point in time, the density of the crust/mantle was so great that no "digger" or subterranean-vehicle could ever dig through the material. When the planet's surface possessed intelligent citizens and modern technology, Digger Vehicles dug through the ground and formed tunnels at the rate of 10 miles a day. There was once a transit system [PEZ candy-shaped vehicles in protective bubbles] under Ceana with cars that attained speeds of 500 miles and hour! Vehicles zoomed on electric cushions and were very comfortable rides for passengers. The underground rail-system was a quick way citizens traveled to other parts of the planet. Of course, that was before the Accelerator and before the Collider. After a certain point in time, the network of tunnels and cars were *crushed* during Dark Ceana's solidification!

The materials of the planet condensed more, got Harder and Harder each time Dark Ceana turned on its axis. And in the very center was a Sphere of Nothing (empty space) that had a diameter of 2000 miles! If you traveled from the surface to the center of Dark Ceana, 3 quarters would be solid and 1 quarter would be empty space.

If the question was asked: *Who lived in this empty sphere on the inside of Dark Ceana?* The logical answer was: No one. Nothing survived the EM Super Energy build up, right? Nothing known in the universe penetrated the new, condensed substance formed by the Mega Energy. Therefore, nothing lived inside the planet, right?

Wrong.

Ceana

Two hundred million EGGS lived and were maintained in the vacuum of the hollow Dark Ceana! It was Her Great Incubator for Her Children of Tomorrow. It was Her Hatchery that preserved and insured EVIL for a long time to come. An iso was not like a human or any other lifeform. They came into our material world by an alternate means. Monitors weren't born or created in laboratories. *They moved through the cracks and seams between molecules* and appeared at will (someone else's Will). The core of Dark Ceana was the perfect place to keep the Queen's "babies" safe. Inside their oval modules, 200,000,000 of them materialized and developed along with their jackets, sunglasses and fedoras.

If Dark Ceana busted apart, shattered to pieces...

The young Monitors still lived! The cold, bloodless creatures would shoot out like pollen exploded from a pollen sack or like a giant human sneezed. Evil would be expanded as a Super Virus and be sent to each star system. Every Monitor Seed would burst from its shell with a job to do: corrupt and destroy everything good and positive in that system. Darkmoor might not have a future for a few reasons. It looked "grim."

***

The future was viewed out of chronological sequence. Jeff Blain was not Jeff Blain anymore. He was another person entirely [DH Jetson] and at a later stage of evolution in his soul-life where he did not care about Teran or Earth movies, music and sports anymore. No, this tiny "god" of a humanoid traveled the "Spaceways" and explored other planets, other dimensions and other times. He had his trusty companion MAX with him, of course. They were inseparable (for a reason). And the dead man also possessed his "Flying Carpet" that carried him and Max *anywhere in the galaxy!*

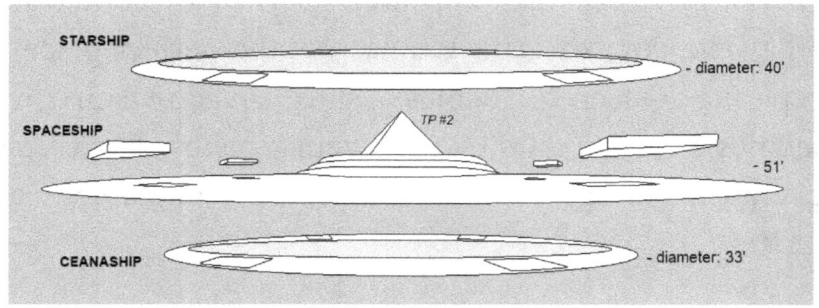

The ship was a *chrysalis* or "crysten" for short. It was another of his inventions. The crysten was 3 ships in one. Passengers were sent to three different locations at the same time. They had the option and visited 3 destinations simultaneously, which depended on where you stepped or stood on the chrysalis. The bottom level did not fly, it smoothly moved along the ground and was a POOL. A programmable pool with a round catwalk that encircled it. Imagine a fast or slow vehicle that whipped through the ground as if it were air! But only the surface of the ground. The "Tub" portion of the crysten moved between molecules, slowly or at lightspeed, but its full range was only the surface of the planet. Along plains, along hills and valleys or along the vertical surfaces of mountains! The Tub section zoomed right along and there wasn't the slightest bump in the ride. There were 4 etched rectangles perfectly spaced on the thin catwalk. When passengers stepped on the rectangles, they were instantly transported to the level above, which was the "Pad" section...

The middle Pad had the largest diameter and *flew*. The circular Pad had a *range of the whole solar system* and was confined to only this solar system. Passengers upon this section could explore any planet or moon in the system, the outer planets, even the four beyond Planet Pluto. No further. If passengers desired to venture out to other star systems, *they stepped on the slabs that hovered in the air.* That immediately brought them to the top section's catwalk, which surrounded a programmable "Bed." It went to any sun system in the galaxy!

Passengers programmed (thought of) where they wanted to go and the Tub, Pad and Bed went off, merrily, to those places in a flash. No whiplash. [Notice the illustration] For example, let's say the Tub was sent to the peak of Mount Everest. You could program the Pool to be a hot-tub or contain any liquid that came to mind, such as raspberry lemonade. If you got bored after minutes of the fabulous view and wanted a change of scenery? You got out and stepped on one of the etched rectangles...now you were on the Pad section (upon one of the blocks) and, let's say, that disk was parked just above the Great Pyramid of Mars and the other pyramids at Cydonia! Neat. Then, from the middle section, you grew tired of the place in an hour and wanted a change? You stepped back on the block in midair and you beamed to the top section's catwalk and found that disk at a different location. Let's say, close to the very colorful and impressive Orion Nebula! You just might want to rest there a minute or two and *drink in* all the cosmic sites, yes? The Bed can be programmed to be any soft material. Notice that if you stepped down from the Bed's catwalk, you landed on top of one of the hovering slabs. From there, you could go either way: step down on the Pad's etched rectangle and go to the Tub section, or jump down elsewhere on Pad's floor and be part of the middle section. Change of destinations depended on which way you stepped.

The middle section contained TP#2. The entity's second Tele-Pyramid. TPs are 4-way transporters (similar to monoliths in the movie 'Time Bandits'). If you grew tired of the 3 locations and wanted to program another reality or go to another Tele-Pyramid in the grid, you thought about it and entered one of the sides of the TP. In fact, large groups of people could use each of 4 doorways [angled pyramid sides] at the same time and all be transported to different, individual locations◇.

TP#1 was located within the entity's 'Fortress of

Solitude' at the high summit of the Shera peak in the center of the lunar Arzachel Crater. TP#3 was positioned on the floor of the big crater, very close to beautiful Eden Lake (crater).

All this was clean and perfect and *impossible*. But it *was* possible if the "entity" that was formerly Jeff Blain thought of it. He was now Anthony Fremont in that Twilight Zone episode with the "cornfield." Not the first one, the movie version where a certain female (angel) guided him toward a better life and a better use of his powers.

|

The man, without his blue aura, had his hand on his ethereal hips and his photonic feet were planted on the middle section of his crysten. The ship was stationary and 3 feet over a particular location on Earth. Bridgeville. Yes, EARTH. It was as photonic as everything else. The wind blew his long, blonde hair. Cook School Woods was on the hill and everything was brand new. You drank water right out of a natural spring. You smelled nature, the earthy smells of the ground and grass and the sweetness of the air. "Aaaah. Nice." He jumped down and impacted the warm soil of Earth. The question was always the same, from moment to moment: *What is there to do?*

Max trailed behind the man, all two-feet of it. It

propelled itself a little faster and fluttered in front of the entity. The man smiled and left it up to the machine, which was part ZED. Max sounded serious with his next words: "I've just recently found a world that opened on Dark Ceana long ago and I think we should explore it, methinks."

"Okay, I trust your judgment, pal. I have a question first, Max?"

"Shoot."

"Why are real experiences we maneuver inside much more intense than imagined ones I dreamed up, eh? Shouldn't they be the same holographic experience?"

The warm (black on the outside) machine answered: "Why is real milk better than powdered milk? Why is a real poncho better than a Sears poncho?"

"Ha. Yer still funny, after all these years..."

"It's my job, it's what I get paid for..."

"Ha, ha. Now what world d'you want us to check out, you Basketball? We don't usually team together in one of my fantasies, you know?"

"This is not like all the sex you do. And by the way, you're gonna lose that little activity in your next stages to come, you know?"

"Really?" the man was surprised.

"Ha, ha. I was kidding. You know, come to think of it: I might want some companionship sometime, like a little friend of my own? A snog-buddy...?"

"Ha, ha. That'd be funny, you have a friend. Like I have you, yer gonna have somebody? Ha, you mean a little Maxie?"

"Yeah. I'll work on it." Then Max's tone changed and it was very serious. "Maybe this new adventure I found is more for *me*, partner, and yer just a tag-along this time? I don't know..."

"That's a switch. Well buddy, if it's important to you, let's do it. What is it now, the world through the cracks?"

"It was originally an M-class planet of the Diadora System, in one of the Magellanic Clouds..."

"That's far," the man commented.

"There was a nuclear war that devastated the planet. Then much later came a global (genetic) disease that wiped out everyone over 16 years old..."

"Really?"

"Yeah, only a few rechargeable devices functioned. Tribes of young people ruled the planet and there wasn't enough food to go around. I shouldn't tell you too much more; it'd ruin the experience. You're one of the children, no more than 12 years old and I'm his faithful robot companion with a limp..."

"Max, yer kidding? And it's not fiction? Okay, what are we about to do?"

"Go into a house and search for food. But not you, *me...*"

"Why just you?"

"They could be booby-trapped. Why have you take the risk when there was...me?"

The man stared at the machine in the air and said, "That's, that's, very brave of you, Max."

"I didn't do it!" the orb yelled. "You think I'd save your Double-Dumb Ass!?"

The man smiled. "Yeah, you would and you have. So. Let's go. I don't know *Why*, but let's go."

"Great. And we're THERE."

|

The boy saw smoke in the air along with Sun rays that broke through patches of thick clouds. This part of the sparse landscape, with trees and a poisoned river, contained only a moderate amount of abandoned houses. There was always a chance that the gangs didn't find everything. Plenty of homes once contained an abundance of food. *Maybe they missed something stored in cans or storage units?*

The boy drank from a tube attached to a small backpack that was an aqua-airator system. When the boy moved or walked, the unit produced a pint of water every 5 hours. The problem was good food, where to acquire it? Strapped to his right shoulder was a Takk rifle and he had a lot of ammunition left, on his chest and belt. The boy found extra ammo from half-eaten soldiers, eaten by mutated wolves in the area. He had shot a few of them as they attacked in the night. He'd never had to gun down a human being and hoped in his heart that it would never come down to that. But he knew that young survivors had become savages, not much more than animals. It was Survival of the Fittest and he was everyone's prey.

In this miserable war-torn and disease-torn world, the boy had one saving grace, one lucky break: he wasn't alone. There was the L8 robot he found. Its memory circuits were badly damaged. It had changed into a simpler kind of android with much less complicated data in its artificial brain. L8 no longer answered complex questions like new models did. The war had basically lobotomized the little mechanical man who stood 3 and a half feet tall and had a round face. The robot was tremendously devoted and attached to the boy. But it made a Big Mistake. It believed the boy was the rich kid that it originally served. That was a few years ago. L8 had limited capacity now, but understood Love. It loved the boy and the boy loved the extremely expensive toy for the rich that its poor family could never have afforded. The boy realized the L8 circuits that were important were still there - they were the places where Love, Compassion and Care were stored. The little robot still possessed those services and they were 100% directed at the boy.

The two of them had been together for 13 months now (the boy counted). It had been a successful campaign. They hid well. L8 often stayed stationary for long periods and still had the sharpest seeing, hearing and other senses. The difference was when it spoke to the boy, it was as if a child spoke. Both were about on the same brain level of sophistication, which was fantastic for the boy. He had a faithful friend. He had a cool little brother. L8 possessed a pronounced limp, but continued steady in its mobility.

The countryside contained many abandoned or blown apart residences separated by forests, mainly. There were also fires from tribes at night. Camps of different colors who were at war and wore warpaint. The boy and L8 had found scattered storage units of good food along the way. Also, houses were found with canned food in the fruit cellars. The boy and droid had been very fortunate. They steered clear of the camps and L8 sounded a low alert if anybody was close.

The problem was they had all the food stored in one

location and their secret spot was *discovered*. Thirteen months of robot-tested food, stored neatly in a safe place, was gone! The duo had to discover another supply and another source quickly. Well, the boy needed it. The robot charged itself and was good to go.

They came upon a house just beyond the last empty house they had examined and decided to proceed...

The robot strongly suggested to the armed boy: "I want a name. Yeah, I want you to call me by a name. Not a number."

He laughed and said, "Alright. What do you want to be called, L8?"

"Late," the round-faced android answered.

"Ha, ha. You want to be called Late? Like late for dinner?"

"That's what I want..."

"Okay," the boy agreed. "Yer late."

"Great."

"You better not be," he joked.

"What?"

"Ha, ha...anyway. Late, what does it look like up ahead?"

They were on a grassy knoll, about 50 feet from a house and there were a lot of trees in the background. Everything was quiet. Part of the roof was missing.

"I don't like it," the machine said. "It's too quiet. Everything is too still."

The boy replied, "The wind stopped."

"No, I have a feeling," Late expressed, sincerely.

"I'm gonna go in," the boy insisted.

"Wait!" Late insisted back. "Please. Please. I'll go in and check it out. Please, sir."

The boy thought about it for a moment. He changed his mind and let his mechanical comrade go in. "Thanks. You're a good friend, Late."

"Pleasure is mine, sir." Late quickly and crookedly walked.

The boy raised the Takk weapon and aimed it in different directions. He kept a sharp bead on the surroundings as the android limped inside. Again, he looked around and saw no one, but he felt something (like being watched). In no time, the robot emerged from the dwelling and marched with a load of canned goods in his metal hands.

He dropped them in front of the boy and said, "There's more."

Ceana

"Good. I'll go in with you..."

"No," Late firmly said. "I can handle it. Feels like we're being seen, although my sensors tell me there is no surveillance on us, no eyes at all..." Late sensed the boy wasn't convinced...

"I'm g..."

"Please! For me. I'll get one more load then we go."

He smiled at the round face and nodded for yes.

The machine with a few missing parts was halfway to the house and the boy said to him: "I love you." It turned and faced the poor boy in tattered clothes and heard: "Late. I wouldn't made it this far if not for you."

It pointed to its chest, then pointed to the boy. Late turned and limped into the house...

Ten seconds later, there was an *explosion!* It took out at least a whole room in the house! Its bright flash and debris were seen out of the roof that wasn't there. The boy watched the roof that caught fire and then the fire spread to the rest of the house. He stayed right there and watched it and knew what had happened. His good Late friend...was not coming out...

|

The future entity of Jeff Blain, which was another person entirely, grabbed the Max orb like it was Jerry

Rice at the Super Bowl! Or, Larry Fitzgerald! Or Lynn Swann! Very, very tightly and cried his little heart out!! Tears dripped down all over the Super Ghost's face. (The man usually made a joke at moments like these).

"You bastard Basketball! I love you, man, *and I'm not even drunk! Why'd you do that? Pull my heartstrings like that?" (sob).

"Hey, that was for me. Why is it always about you, eh? You, you, you, it's always about YOU. It's what you want, never me? You have a big fur coat at home? Love me, love me! Look at me!"

"Stop doing Seinfeld. No one gets him anymore. So Max, sum it up. What's the lesson here?"

The warm Basketball, sometimes Beach Ball, stated plainly: "When you reach higher Levels of your Afterlife you will know what is truly important and you know what that is. You've felt it all your life, Mister Jetson."

***

"Cozy little place you have here," Dan Hegel Jetson lied as he looked around where Jain and Dorsey "bunked" on the protected base that orbited Dark Ceana. "I like it." The artificial environment was bleak, cold, purely functional and unattractive. "Not much space. A bit spartan. Could use a few throw pillows. That was from 'Young Frankenstein.' I'll show it to you sometime. Good movie. Lotta great lines. You'll laugh. It's very important to laugh, Jain. And 'Duck Soup,' that's a good one too. Yeah, but I have to stop with the references..."

"Where's Dorsey?"

Jetson looked into the Detective's eyes and said, "I thought it'd be better if it was just you and me, kid." He fell to the cold, hard floor that contained a very thick and modern comforter plus a zippered sleeping mattress. It cushioned his fall and there was another one next to it.

Jain did the same and fell down on the other bed. She smiled. She sat. She was all-ears and wanted to hear every word the magic man said.

He asked, "I don't see your associate, the Andorian. Shouldn't he be here?"

Jain replied, "I guess he left through the stargate."

Jetson said, "Don't look now, babe, but I don't see that lil' stargate of yours anywhere around these tight quarters. How'd he take it with 'em, eh? Wait, I smell a bigger mystery here. Why are there only two beds when this space was shared by three?"

"You're sitting on mine and Dorsey's..."

"I know, I know! I wrote you guys as gay, but I don't know if you're a full-blown lesbian from Lesbos Island or bi-sexual? I left it up to you. Which is it? Cough it up, c'mon, not much time, kid."

Jain had him for sure, just like she surprised the Angel. She expressed, "I fucked the Heart Center, the *bright* one!"

Dan jumped to his feet like a bomb went off inside and repeatedly pushed a...

"Truth button! Truth button! Max! Max! This is what happens when one of these story-monkeys runs amok!"

The Max-screen/PEZ machine materialized, all 156 inches, and it perfectly fit in the width of the orbiting base, very snug. "Ugh," it grunted.

"...Sidebar, (to Jain) the width of space here is only 156 inches. And *this* was where I wanted to meet? Your *shagging*-spot was much better, but that's not the point." (seriously) "How d'you ever get to boink the leader of the Rangers?? Ha, the head COP! It's like doing Dudley Do-Right if he was a god, ha!" Mister Jetson was truly mystified and was all-ears.

"It wasn't a shagging-spot. For a while, a long time ago, I was like a groupie..."

"Bet you were hot once."

"I'm still hot," Jain fired back. "...and I did the lead singer of a band I saw. I thought he looked like a famous pro Roval player. I was in love. God, could he play guitar. But he told me we had no future because he was

really an alien and very, very tiny. He was moonlighting, see, having fun with the band and he needed a break from all of his superhero duties..."

"Wow. Wowie. This is all freaking news to me; I didn't write this. Huh." Dan was amazed. "So, it was like you fucked Clark Kent?"

Jain confessed, "Yeah, yeah, sure. The Heart Center showed me a few tricks I won't go into. He was an alien alright. Ha, ha. I've never forgotten. But I had to. He blotted it out to the world. I've kept the secret until now, uh, er, what do I call you?"

"Dan. Call me, Dan. Well, there's another loose end resolved. Yer like an iso you, I mean I, can't control, huh? I'm gonna find out why, someday." The man turned to the screen. "Hi, Max. Jain, this is Max. You wanted to know everything, you said? Then Max is the guy you wanna see. He knows everything. He's like God."

"But I'm still learning," the screen said. "Strange paradox."

Dan gave Max the lead-in set up for a joke: "Jain's a detective..."

"You mean she's a dick?"

"She sure is." Man and machine had a good laugh.

"That was so funny. You guys should take the act on

the road (sarcasm). Hi, Max." She waved. Jain was in good spirits. Her 'spider-senses' were at ease. She joked: "Now it's even smaller in here, thanks."

Max transmitted: "I like her...DJ."

Jain said, "I almost thought Max was going to say: 'Captain,' for some reason."

"Interesting," Dan replied. "Movie time!"

She responded, "Oh? We're going to watch a movie, is that right?"

Dan Jetson corrected himself: "Not a movie. It's hard to explain, Jain. What you'll see is the future; this is a window into the future. It hasn't happened yet, a point I haven't gotten to yet, but I will. I got to view this recording, so I already know what's gonna happen later in my Afterlife..."

She added, "But that will change the situation when you get there since you already know what's going to happen?"

"Exactly."

"Where's that leave us?" she asked in a semi-desperate tone.

He joked: "Not in East McKeesport. I'll put it to ya this way, Jainy: You know how we were all worried and agonized about potential Doomsday? You, everyone in

Darkmoor, viewers, readers, watchers, listeners, and even me? A Collider out-of-control that increased daily in Power and no one can pull its Plug?! Splitting Reality? Colliding Worlds Together? The, the, new Paradise-Planets that for sure were going to collapse with the increased Super Energy, remember? And, and, certainly Dark Ceana had to electrically/magnetically BLOW to smithereens soon, right, Miss Detective? A Galactic Power Outage, Blown Fuse?! We're a little too close to the MEGA BOMB, right? And. Isn't it time for the Grand Finale...?"

"Yeah," she wasn't sure about her answer.

"...And two million evil Monitors will be jettisoned far into the galaxy when that happens, aye?"

"Huh?" Jain knew nothing about the: "Monitors?"

"Oh, wait! That's a *real* threat and has to be resolved in the real world, actually. Oh, God. I'm mixing my Doomsdays, that's worse than metaphors. Forget all the ultimate disasters, Okay? Forget all the fears and worries. Just be cool and casual because none of those bad things are going to happen to us, Jain."

"Why? Because you decided not to write it that way, God?"

DJ rolled his eyes. "I'm not God! *'Although'*...that's just a big BUT, I am the Director of this little play, ah, what would you call it? I wear many hats: writer, producer, director. What did they call it in Star Trek?" He looked at the Max-screen.

It transmitted: "Upstart."

"Ha, ha," Dan laughed. [Jain didn't]. "You know that's not the word, you little bastard. Ha." (to Jain) "Surprise is very important, like Inspector Clouseau and the little yellow guy. Did I ever tell you how important it is to be funny? Wrote two books on the subject, joke books, I just found out. I haven't read them yet. And I think there's a third funny book coming? Yeah, I'm a bloody author! Who knew? Glad I'm not a reporter..."

Max relayed the proper word from Star Trek: "Menagerie."

"That's it. A little slow, Max," Jetson pointed. "Menagerie. I am god of this menagerie."

She inquired, "And I'm a part of your menagerie?"

"*Mmom,* ah, ya, kind of. Would you rather have oblivion? That's what I just found out not too long ago. You're all characters of mine...and, and, that includes ME! But I digress. Like I said, it's *Movie Time*, yes? I even have 'ectoplasmic popcorn' for you to consume. Yummy, buttered..."

Jain remembered and said, "And this window into the future is important and will explain things to me?"

"You're the one who wanted the truth. Me too, kid, we're related that way. We're all walking our own paths to Veritas, to the Halls of Elaraa. You won't believe where I got that from. We're all in our own Roval Match. It's similar to the end of 'Betelgeuse.' Different for everyone. It's like I was an apprentice to a Master, and now you're my apprentice, Jain..."

She asked, "Who was your Master?"

The Max-screen answered, "Me."

"Oh, God," she reacted.

"Almost. Also, when you see me in the future...I'm, uh, how would I say it? I'm a much more happy and excited and more emotional version of me than the cool Daniel Hegel Jetson that you see before you today. I'm always changin', ha. Like Bowie. Okay? Any questions?"

Jain had every question in the universe, but she shook her head for *no*. The lights dimmed and the show had begun...

|

"Wow!! And wow, wow, wowie!! *This is my ship?!* You touched the side of my head and now I understand exactly how to operate the chrysalis?!"

"You call it a crysten, Mister Jetson," Aan, the Warmth, replied.

"Call me, Dan," (no longer Jeff) the humanoid entity shook with supreme delight. There were tears of joy in his big eyes.

"For now." A few seconds later, the Angel accessed and said, "So what would you little maniac like to do first?"

"Ha, ha, ha. Aan, *you have a sense of humor.* That was from a movie."

She smiled and her aura brightened.

"Well, I'll tell ya, toots. How's about we check out my base on the Moon? *Yay.* Coming?"

"Wouldn't miss the look on your face...Dan."

The man was ecstatic and had to run through the "tour" that was recently programmed into his head. On the Pad section of the crysten, he jumped 3 steps up to where Tele-Pyramid #2 was positioned, in the central heart of the 51-foot disk. He asked, "Yer saying...I invented this, designed it?"

Aan stepped upon each of the three steps and stood next to him. She replied, "We picked it out of your mind and made it function for you. The same can be said for the Tele-Pyramid System you created. You're the Creator."

"Neat. Ah, ah, crap, I, I don't know what to say to

you. Ah...*thanks*. There's one thing I don't understand..."

"Only one?" She smiled again.

"I think that's my joke. And when I know that, I'll forget everything else, eh? I'll start again: I don't see what you and all the other Archon ghosts get out of this. You help us; you've given me and many others so much. What do you get out of it?"

"You don't know? We use you. When you dream and fantasize, we maneuver inside the images and the sensations you produce. We're not as selfless as you believe."

"I'm a drug!"

"Ha, ha." She pointed at the angled side of the TP. "You know what to do..."

"Yeah. We have to hold hands and go in together 'cos of the time warp, right?"

"Right as rain, Daniel Jetson," She grabbed his hand.

DJ asked, "Now if I want to see my base at the top of Arzachel, I don't have to say 'TP one,' I can say 'one' and it's programmed?"

Warmth told him: "You need not speak words. Think *ONE*, and the system knows where you want to go, the door will open. Practice thinking your commands."

"Wow." His eyes widened and his heart raced a bit faster. It would be the first time the man traversed a Vortex like a Star Gate. "Let's go!" He pulled her in and they were both *softly sucked* inside! As soon as they were propelled inside the 7 and a half-foot tall Tele-Pyramid, IT SPIT OUT DAN AND A FLYING BLACK SPHERE!!

Dan wore different colored clothes, had different colored hair (blue) and had a different hairstyle. He collapsed and fell down the three white [crystalene] steps and in a total state of rapture! [The dead man could not get hurt or feel physical pain]. He stretched out on the floor of his wonderful, wonderful *flying carpet*. Dan blubbered to himself: "And, and...it's all mine? I can go, go anywhere, see anything, like, like, I'm the...Captain...? Ha. I remember. Like the Thief of Bagdad! What, no Magic Cloak?"

|

Jain swallowed 'popcorn,' raised her hand and had questions. Max understood and paused the film. "Hold on, what was that 'time warp' he said? *You* said?! And now you have different hair and a different colored outfit a split second later? Did my eyes just witness a time warp? And what the hell was that spooky black ball that shot out?"

"That would be me...again," the Max-screen and PEZ Machine answered.

Dan Jetson calmly replied, "Your eyes did indeed observe a time warp, Jain. We do the 'time warp' 'round here. It's just a step...Yes, the spooky black ball is this guy, my best friend. I sense you're catching on...?"

"What the heck happened in the time I didn't see?"

"Show 'er, Max. Play it again, Max," Dan ordered like he was in Casablanca.

|

The wide screen displayed Dan, then Aan, and they were gently *pushed forward* out of an angled side of Tele-Pyramid #1 at the pinnacle of the Shera tower (mountain). The panoramic view was super extraordinary from the crater to the far reaches of the lunar landscape and to the bright blue horizon, ultimately. Tremendous colors! There was a subtle rain of pink raindrops. Light-purple clouds. The ever-changing sky was a very deep violet at zenith during this particular time of late evening. But it was the phenomenal ~FEELINGS~ that were felt in this amazing location (of the mind) that were most memorable.

Dan never saw a scene like what was in front of him before and he was a nervous wreck. *He dreamed what he could do with a vehicle like this and a companion like Max at his side!* When the man handled his emotions better, he walked to the edge of the high base and gazed down upon the floor of his crater. He saw Eden Lake. It was the brightest turquoise color his eyes had ever seen. Arz's [ours] floor was a deep yellow-orange color. Dan wiped his face and expressed, "I'd like to visit the lake..."

She tenderly said, "I'll stay here." Aan smiled once more.

He thought the number: *THREE*, and walked in and instantly exited the TP at lakeshore a few miles down below.

Aan went to the edge, looked down and saw him at the shore of Eden. Each had keen eyesight. They waved. The man spent minutes in an out of perfect waters while a light rain sprinkled on top of him. He returned, *gently urged* out of TP#1. He faced his Angel and was totally silent. He absorbed the whole experience of the last minutes and was deeply humbled by everything. Dan Jetson took a giant breath. With a thought, he changed his hair and outfit to a cooler look. He was beyond tears at the moment. He compartmentalized his strong feelings, for now. Later, he'd explore the stars<>.

She surprised him with the words: "I will leave you to your ship, Captain..."

"You're going?" Dan sounded sad.

She said, "Don't worry, I'll be watching. There's someone you should get used to as you travel the Spaceways. You're a lot alike. Bye. And thank you,

Mister Jetson."

Aan was gone and in her place was...

"Max! Hey, you bouncing ball, isn't the crysten *cool*? And before you ask, no, you can't drive it."

After the black-on-the-outside orb materialized in midair, it questioned: "What do you mean? There's three sections to it. *I can't drive one of the disks?*"

"Oh, yeah, yeah, I'm not thinkin' clearly right now, pal. I should go back to Bridgeville. There's something I want to check out in my old man's fruit cellar..."

"I'm with you," the machine said.

"Let me take another gander at this place before I go, eh?" Dan looked in all directions. "Wow and wowie, eh? It's a heck of a Fortress of Solitude, huh, Max?"

"No kidding, boss."

They both slipped back into a side of TP#1 and were *propelled out* of TP#2 on the crysten, which was parked a few feet over the backyard of 794 Bower Hill Road.

Max-screen stopped the video and explained to Jain: "Yes, your eyes saw only a split-second difference from when they went in...and when Dan came out. He looked different and faced the other way, then fell down the steps, happy. The *tour* he took, to him, in that split-second of yours, actually lasted close to 14 minutes..."

"Imagine that." Jain was thrilled by the new knowledge and the new scenes.

Max commented, "Boy did Dan gush with emotions, huh, Jain? You weren't too cool then, Captain Crybaby..."

"Hey, hey, hey, you're the upstart, and I'm right here in the room. (to Jain) But there's much more to the movie I want to show you, Jain."

"Do it," she said, pleased as punch, with a big smile on her face.

"Max..." Dan directed.

|

The future scene was a location that was considered *the most beautiful beach in the solar system!* It was on a very large planet that was the last planet in our solar system (Baradoom), the 13th. DH Jetson with sunglasses laid on a blanket and was close to the water's edge. Reports were true. Maybe another spot that went around some other star was lovelier than this, but that was hard to imagine. With help from his Flying Carpet and Max, he wanted to find out. *Wonder what he's doin' right now?*

Then, suddenly, Aan appeared and she formed clothes on Dan with a snap of her fingers. She asked a question she knew the answer to: "Are the girls gone?"

"You have impeccable timing, Aan. Ha. Yes, the girls are all gone, ha, ha."

"Ha, ha. Well, dear boy, I promised you the truth. That I would one day bring you to the truth, yes? Didn't I?"

"Since I'm never going to be *enlarged*, you might as well hit me with the truth, kid. It's what I've (we) been waiting for. Whatcha got?"

Suddenly, books rained down upon the man. Books. Paperback books exactly 6 inches by 9 inches in size and of various thicknesses, 18 of them. They fell out of a clear and fabulous sky^.

"What the hey? What's this? You want me to read books? *I'm on vacation.* What kind of books are these?"

She replied, "Mostly stories. Isn't everything only stories? The news. The future. Even ancient history. It's just recorded stories."

"Nice covers. Is this homework? Am I gonna be tested on these books?"

"No, not at all," she replied. "I think you'd like them, though. Learn something, you know, get smarter? They're pretty wild. Pay close attention to the ones entitled: 'The Mandela Effect' and also 'Pez Wars' and

'The PEZ-Effect.'"

"PEZ?"

"Oh, Dan," she especially remembered. "...And if you want to *laugh*, did you know it's very important to laugh? Then read two of the books, they'll be a third one maybe, written by a fellow named *DH Jetson*. Yeah, that's his name, Jetson."

"What? Gimme that, no, gimme that, no, gimme that, *there it is!* Jetson, eh? My jokes, ha! I'll be. I'll bet they're very funny. I'm a real comedian, you know? People always said I was funny. Say Aan, who's this Caladan guy?"

"You are. TS Caladan has a cool anagram you will appreciate: At Scandal. TS Eliot, the famous writer, has a terrible anagram that was also significant: toilets."

The man didn't really hear her and was lost by the name. "Caladan, Caladan, better than Calaban. Wait." He remembered. "That's from Dune! The water-world, before they went to Arrakis, they were on Caladan." Then her words clicked in his brain. "This is real? Oh, oh, that's why yer showing me the books, *I wrote them?* Ah! Wait. I don't remember that. When the hell did I write them? I'm dead!"

"It was another you from another timeline."

"Really? Huh. Still cool. Hey, I was an author, not

just a musician. Wow. Are they good, was I famous?"

She replied, "Your later ones are good and no...you were not famous."

"Why was that?"

"Because that other you was not fortunate. He did not fare too well in life. He was not as lucky as you were and are, my son."

"I'm sorry to hear that..."

|

"There's only one or two more scenes that you should see," Jetson said to Jain. (to Max) Don't you just love it when everything comes together in the end, such precision, huh?" Dan grabbed a handful of the unreal popcorn and munched.

"I'll play it for you now, folks," Max said with a spring in its voice.

"Do it," the man said.

|

Dan was engrossed by the books, especially the art. *He must have had help. The computer did the art.* The video displayed a montage of a nude and semi-nude Mister Jetson as he read books he'd written but never seen before. He read them in order while he utilized the different disks of his 3-way ship: a) He read a few from his Tub section that sped smoothly through the surface of Bonneville Salt Flats. b) He skimmed a bunch of the old books while at the summit of the Martian Olympus Mons. Dan discovered that the fantastic vistas that surrounded him were secondary compared to the words credited to him. *Who was this guy?* Dan was a musician and enjoyed the visual arts. Writing was not his thing. c) And then he came to 'Pez Wars.' He flipped out and relaxed on the silkiness of his Bed section while it flew just beyond the Crab Nebula Supernova! "Oh, my FRIGGEN GOD!! HAAAA~ Well, this is a sweet surprise..."

Dan didn't think they made PEZ candy anymore. He didn't collect PEZ dispensers. But, in all other respects, he was the main character. He was Jeff Blain! "I have no conscious memory of writing this, but I recognize so many personal things in Book 1 and 2, it's like I really was the main character. Huh. And I wrote my own story?"

|||

Later, Dan laid in Jain's bed, inside her cool/clear sphere whose bottom was slapped by waves at high tide from the Pax Ocean. She wasn't around. He always wanted to inspect her fantastic place he wrote for her, in detail, intimately. Now he had the chance. Sexy boudoir. The view of the beach and ocean from within the clear sphere was incredible. Most everyone on (what was)

Ceana had individually-styled domes. Jain had to be different and lived inside two domes put together, which stood upon clear legs on a secluded beach (Malibu, not Catalina). "Love the blue bushes."

Max was in the bedroom also and had a lot of questions, too many questions for Jetson who was very comfortable in Jain's luxurious, round waterbed. He started to read 'Ceana' and he was interrupted by Max, again and again. He was extremely anxious to read it - Max bothered him - *and he sternly told Max to "Shut-up!"* Max stood in midair, did not move and had not said a word since. It was their First Fight.

Dan said he was *very sorry* to his constant companion. Maybe they needed a little space? But there was nothing that he could say or do to change the orb's brain. Max obeyed his Master and did not say one word to the man. A minute of silence....

"The silent treatment, eh? And yer gonna just hover there, motionless? Okay, be that way! It's a free country. I have a book to read, partner. Now, where was I...?"

Unexpectantly, Max said: "My oath of silence starts now..."

"I told you, no Seinfeld. Okay, now. Sssh...(speed-read)...Anthill reference was from '5th Element.' OMG! My games! I've tried to get people interested in them for the last 20 years and zilch! 'Attack ships on fire off the shoulder of Orion' was what Rutger Hauer said at the end of 'Bladerunner.' Glittering C-beams near Tannhauser Gate. There's no such thing as C-beams! F-beams, sure. Hmm, the eclipse will mean something. Ah, the truth is *shadowed* in the Media. Must be Shadowday. Ha. Woah, I wrote that there were three Ziggurats left after the War, then I wrote there were only two? What a blatant mistake; hope nobody caught it, eh? Elaraa was from 'Watership Down' and I misspelled it. God, this is all out of Star Wars: 'Then he will surrender to me.' This guy (me) isn't original at all. And isos are from the remake of 'Tron,' unplanned lifeforms that just appeared in the computer matrix. Gee, wonder why 'Arz' was used? It's only been my fantasy, safe, 'happy place' ever since high school! 'Facade,' that's not a real band, that's my band. My music. I'm starting to remember, maybe I did write this? Spectre, spelled the British way...so Bond. I used my turned-off phone # for the Hover-Capsule #. Huh, Rose was my mother's name. The MONITORS, wait, wait, that was from a movie I saw way back in the '60s. A comedy with the green Star Trek girl, only she wasn't green. There were these Monitors, I think, aliens that wore bowler hats. Not ties, sunglasses and fedoras. Wow, that came out of me? Ha, 'mostly harmless.' This guys steals everything and it's me. At least 'Narchons' sounded original. I've used blue chlorophyll before. Aliens always staying away from water were the creeps in 'Dark City.' Huh, bald and in black. Gee..." He turned to Max who remained motionless and silent. "When I first wrote the Monitor who came from behind the curtains, I had no idea that was Dark Heart Center, under his bloodless skin. Later, it hit me: *Yeah,* make him the Devil, opposite of the Ranger leader. It worked out. I DO remember this! Then the whole CERN-thing comes in. 'The Day Ceana Stood Still,' *wonder where that came from?* That's a real quote, Ceana means 'God is Merciful,' then I Forrest Gumped it. Tannhauser Gate used again. Thank you, Rutger. I keep reusing 'Phantom Menace.' Where'd 'Stripe' come from? *Ghoulies!* No, it was Gremlins! That's it. Sure have written enough about Arzachel; is that why I got it? Max? Still not talkin', eh? Okay. Of course, the crater colony had to be called 'Escher.' 'Tears in the Rain,' that's more Rutger Hauer from the end of 'Bladerunner.' Right Max? You know, Max, knowing everything takes the mystery out of life. [nothing]. God, this is deep. 'Interview with a Monitor' is 'Interview with a Vampire,' which is a Mandela-Effect or PEZ-Effect. Soul-transfer, my ex-wife did that. This is better than 'Solaris,' an ever-changing planet. Jain went to the same crater tower that Heart went to...and it's *my* crater. Wow. Yeah, I never talk to myself. Why would I ever talk to me? Yes, we are being canceled. The 'Great Escarpment.' Had to call the curvy lines something. I think I'm in love with Jain, Max. Her bed smells fantastic." (Looked over) Still nothing. "Okay, where was I? Ah. See, I made sure I didn't wear a beard. You know how many dudes wear beards today? *All of them!* I have to be an individual, a rebel, it's like my signature. I wanna play Roval so badly. I need a partner. I mean one with hands. 'Not seen' the inevitable, that was a reverence to 'Nazi.' OMG, 'If you put a bullet in a furnace, it'll explode' is from Bill Cosby. Ha. What the hell did the white bird mean? There's a loose end I never followed up on. Could've made it a dead Archon. Oh, well. 'Multi-Pass,' that's another '5th Element' reference. The # used for the systems that tapped the Power is my Social Security #, minus a digit. Ha. And 101 is the number of PEZ dispensers I have right at this moment, *but I thought I didn't collect them?* Ah...that was the other guy. Two minds. Right. I remember that cold fruit cellar, it was real. Wasn't it 'cellar door' in 'Donnie Darko'? That was like a 'One Step Beyond.' Huh, that's my old address on Bower Hill Rd. And I even mentioned Cook School Woods and the spring. Memories. Reality is long gone, but the memories will never go away. Still-Suits! That's from 'Dune,' but mine were different. The story sure went sideways..." When Dan viewed (read) real scenes, only they were inspired from the artwork of Simon Stalenhag, he said: "Where have I seen this imagery before...?"

"Ha."

"Did I hear something from the Peanut Gallery?" Dan Jetson wondered.

Max went back to the silent treatment.

"I see. Now where was I after I was so rudely interrupted?" The man remained upset at his flying friend. But when Dan read and maneuvered and felt the feelings between the 12-year old child without a name and the small, faithful android who wanted to be called 'Late'...*he broke down and cried his little heart out!* He leaped off the comfy waterbed and air-tackled the beautiful, black orb. "I'm so sorry, mate. (sob) Whatever would I do without you? Interrupt me anytime, my man. I love you."

"I love you too, you knucklehead. Ha, ha. You shudda said: '*Oh*, shut-up,' eh?"

"Right, then it's Okay. Yeah. Sometimes I am a knucklehead. I have to sincerely say this: Max, I wouldn't made it this far if not for you."

Max *cried* inside, but did not show it. He realized immediately where the quote came from. The lovely machine confessed: "Honestly, I need something to do. Don't worry. I'll find a hobby, a project, and it won't involve you. Always you, huh? Ha, ha."

"Great." Dan smiled a very big smile.

Now the feelings in the clear sphere were wonderful.

"Gotta go. Call me if you need me and we'll go someplace together, boss..."

"Like at the end of Mead?"

"Right." Max disappeared.

The man was in a tizzy and a dizzy of weird thoughts. He recalled: "I forgot to use 'Death found a way' and to bring in another Ceanaquake, hmm. Also 'star-making,' I could have had them *Build Suns* so there'd be more stars in the night sky. That didn't happen. Ceana, originally, was an island in another story of mine and the concept was the same. And what happened to a 'PEZ Planet' I was gonna flesh-out? Also, didn't happen. But maybe, somewhere it did? How 'bout that?"

Dan fell back onto the soft, round bed that moved. He closed his eyes. He thought of Aan. He felt she, or his mother, won't be around for too much longer either, but they'd watch and care and protect. He received a mental image from her (them) and it was similar to the robot's goodbye to the boy in real history. He saw her point to her heart...and then she pointed back towards him. Dan Jetson felt the love. Then...

Suddenly, *Jain beamed in!* She was a little shocked by the arrival and that her bedroom had been invaded. She looked great. Blonde hair. Nice. She thought: *Just barge right in, why don't you?* The girl could have gotten angry. Instead...she smiled.

DHJ smiled back, raised his arms up and said,

"Surprise. Hi, Jainy. Here's a funny one: I was gonna make you preggers with the Heart's baby only I decided, no."

"Thanks a lot."

***

Much later, I asked Max about his new friend ["his" and not "its"] and his reply was: *"Now I can't get rid of the cute little guy.* I've created a monster. *It lives.* He loves me! Can't be 'cos of my good looks. Must be my sparkling personality, HA! Maybe I make him laugh?"

"Hey, Max. Have you noticed that you are a lot like me when we first met and I'm much like you...when we first met?"

"No." He thought about it again. "I think yer wrong 'bout that, Charlie," the soft/warm orb said.

"And you have a different shape to you now, little thingees on you. Funny, I got you for a companion and now you have little Remmy as a companion. HA! You have a BABY! I didn't even know you were pregnant, son. Sorry I wasn't there for the birth. Aaaaww. Yer buddy yer so attached to, and it's so nice you have a little friend now..."

"He's attached to me," Max corrected the man.

"...Why do you call 'em 'Rem'? Because of REM sleep?"

"No, he's a *fucking remora!* I can't get rid of him! I told ja, eh? Oh, shit. Here comes the little bugger now. He's so damn cute, I know. Ah. I hafta go." ~~~

"Ha, ha, ha." DH Jetson laughed after his old friend disappeared. "You don't fool me for a second, you Beach Ball! You love the attention. When I'm away, yer bored, eh? 'Cos you have nothing to do, right? I had a cat like that. Why is it so hard for you to make something up? You know, DO SOMETHING! I do it all the time. *Oh, you did,* with Rem. Now I get it. That was your project, I see. Man, I am slow. You know you guys are *in love, eh?* That's like marriage. I have to say it right: Maawedge. Ha."

Jetson was given a view of when Max was at his happiest. The happiest moment in his very long and lovely, mechanical life. A ZEDNAR that knew everything and still learned and felt new sensations because of humans. Max's greatest moment was when he and Rem maneuvered within a real situation from Earth and shared an extraordinary Undersea Kingdom. *It was like when I caught baseball with dad. Beautiful. Perfect.*

Ceana

***

No matter what was true, what were dreams, what was holographic or what was only a story in a book...

There remained a major problem in the real world: CREEPS. It was an actual threat and not a fictional one. Negative bastards that wanted to screw everything up that was good and decent. Pricks. Isos had only grown in power over the last generation. Evil was everywhere and nowhere and could not be destroyed. Not by normal means. How do you fight an Enemy that was everywhere? We watched and believed the news on our Tele-Screens, but our Tele-Screens never informed the public of the *true Enemy* and that Tele-Screens were one of the biggest weapons used by humanity's Hidden Enemy. How can the spread of Darkness and Wrongness be contained or stopped in a dystopian world? Creepy isos (minions of Evil) were on the network channels, were given television shows, starred in movies, were given big record contracts, did computer and commercial ads and also lived across the street.

THEY LIVE! Not everyone in society. There were plenty of kind, generous, thoughtful human beings on Earth. [But who was IN Earth?]. Where were we headed in the future? What will Tomorrow really bring? Hasn't the light of truth been snuffed out more and more over recent years? Hasn't the Darkness of Lies and Deception been hailed and promoted just about everywhere we looked and in all forms of Media? And, the Ultimate Question: **Who created the Earth Collider that reversed our world?**

Maybe there was a magical, metaphysical way to trap THE DEVIL? To keep him and all of his minions (eggs) imprisoned behind bars like in the Twilight Zone episode with John Carradine? It's a metaphor. Sometimes prayers worked...

What happened to the Monitor creeps in the 'Ceana' story, Men in Black isos that defied logic and physics? Were they harbingers of the Final Doomsday? Were they Mothmen? Who created them? Who sent them to this galaxy? Were the bald fuckers in fedoras the start of all the problems in the first place? Time told us that they were and they had to be dealt with in the true sense so that no other galaxy in the cosmos would ever be similarly affected by the spread of dark forces from dark dimensions...

By extraordinary means, in a Timeless Realm, the Universe contained them all and turned them into one particular kind of PEZ dispenser that was most appropriate. The adult and child versions of Monitors were neatly <u>locked</u> behind a single display case that will *never be opened*. Now, it was the eyes of the world that watched the Watchers. The Universe was reasonably sure that an entire galaxy would never be annihilated, before the time when all the galaxies were supposed to be annihilated. Galactic Doom would not happen again. But... *[Do not open the case!]*.

The End

TS Caladan

TS Caladan

Tray Caladan was born Doug Yurchey in Pittsburgh, PA. in 1951 to Rose and Stephen Yurchey. A shy, only-child retreated into his own world and drew pictures. He earned a tennis scholarship to Edinboro State as an art major only to quit and begin the 'Art Trek' gallery. He married a psychic (Katrina) that would forever change his life and send him on a course to solve great mysteries. In 1990-91, he worked as a background clean-up artist on the 'Simpsons.' Tray's important articles, books, videos, radio shows, theories, patent, stories, ideas, games and art can be viewed online. His positive message of a "New Human Genesis" from Mars and ancient technology based on the work of Nikola Tesla permeates his theories and research as well as his "Science Fiction" and life.

TSCALADAN@gmail.com Contact author, comments/questions are welcome.

Find links to all his e-books and paperbacks at www.twbpress.com/authortraycaladan.html.